Italian Millionaire, Runaway Principessa

SUN CHARA

A division of HarperCollins*Publishers*
www.harpercollins.co.uk

HarperCollins
PUBLISHERS
Since 1817

Harper*Impulse* an imprint of
HarperCollins*Publishers*
1 London Bridge Street
London SE1 9GF

www.harpercollins.co.uk

A Paperback Original 2017

First published in Great Britain in ebook format by Harper*Impulse* 2017

A catalogue record for this book
is available from the British Library

ISBN: 9780008145057

Typeset in Minion by Palimpsest Book Production Ltd, Falkirk, Stirlingshire

Printed in Great Britain

*Unlimited thanks to my wonderful brother, Joseph
who is quantum leaps ahead of his time ...
you are an inspiration!*

*Greatest gratitude and admiration to all the people
(including my brother Joseph) in the medical field for
your courage, dedication, and heroic efforts in
saving lives! I applaud you!*

Chapter 1

Peter saw her. And he saw men at the bar ogling her every curve. The waitress scrap-of-nothing she wore accentuated the length and shape of her legs, clad in net stockings. How she managed to walk on stiletto heels was beyond his male comprehension. The flimsy froth of fabric barely covered her bottom and had her breasts nearly spilling from the Grand Canyon neckline, to the delight of every male eye in the smoke-filled room.

He brushed rain-damp hair off his brow, warring with his gut instinct to stride over, sling her across his shoulder, and take her home. Hot blood surged through him and his aorta boxed his chest. Home where she belonged, with him, and in his bed—

The crash of glass jolted him from plunging deeper into the erotic fantasy. Since she'd run out on him, his mind was set on replay … a constant rankling to his Italian pride.

A muscle assaulted his jaw. Her rebellious escapade could bring him down, and her with him. Premeditated or a case of the lamb amidst wolves? His chest constricted. It was time to set the record straight, even the score. Although he had to move fast to snare the *coup d'état* he was after, he'd do it his way. He inhaled, filling his lungs with needed oxygen and grimaced at the smoke-tainted air in the club. He exhaled and snared her in his narrow focus.

She was floundering to pick up broken glass from the floor. Her admirers were moving in, but in two long strides he was beside her. The spinning strobe light cast a halo around her, making her hair gold and her skin a shimmer of silk. Memories rushed in, taunting, smothering … and he almost changed his mind. Passion and anger raged inside him. Pent-up pressure in his chest sizzled between his teeth and banished the past, but only for the moment.

"Let me help you." He hunkered down, playing knight gallant, but feeling more like a Neanderthal. His words held a double meaning for this woman, who kept a special place in his heart, his life, and who had spurned his every effort. Why would she have left him otherwise? Without a word, without a backward glance?

The deep timbre of the man's voice filtered to Ellie through the music and laughter, but she kept her head bent until the embarrassed blush receded from her features. "Thank you."

He dropped a handful of sharp pieces onto her tray, and the gold cufflink on his white shirt cuff gleamed from beneath the dark sleeve of his jacket. His hand was strong, his fingers long and sensitive, with a smattering of black hair across his knuckles.

She swallowed and glanced up, her heart splitting in two. "Pet-e-r."

His raised eyebrow spoke volumes.

"What are you doing here?" She held the tray between them like a defense, gripping it so tight her fingers hurt. Her stomach lurched; air whooshed from her lips and every fiber of her being buzzed with life on seeing him again. But with that came a profound sadness.

She turned away from his penetrating blue gaze. His relentless pursuit of his profession had nearly destroyed her and their marriage. She couldn't go back to him. Wouldn't.

Not unless he was willing to change … give her what she wanted, what she … they … deserved … a real marriage. Tears stung her eyelids, and she gulped them down with her next breath.

A melody drifted to her, a balm to her frazzled emotions. She'd been stagnating, except in the bedroom. And she wanted to be more to him than a bedroom playmate. In a desperate attempt to reclaim her life, and save her marriage, she had made a rash decision and fled.

She was playing a risky card, especially since he controlled the deck. Could she pull it off? Would he ever see her as more than a possession?

"Better question is" – he dropped a chipped martini glass on her tray, shattering her thoughts – "what're you doing here, Ellie?"

He reached out to help her up, but she avoided his gesture and stood up on her own. It was doubtful a man like Peter, with a heritage steeped in tradition, would budge, even for her … or her father. Forgiveness was not one of his tendencies.

"Working." She made to pass him and the broken goblets rattled precariously on the tray.

He blocked her path, his gaze gliding over her half-exposed breasts, then lower, taking in the full length of her. "So I see."

She drew in a sharp breath. "I don't like what you're implying, Peter."

"What's that?" he baited.

"That I'm—I'm—"

"Selling favors?"

"How dare you," she snapped, raising a hand to slap him.

He intercepted it in mid-air, his fingers shackling her wrist. "How dare I?" His face was a thundercloud and his eyes bore into her. "You're the one who deserted—"

"I did not."

"No?"

"It wasn't like that."

"Suppose you tell me how it was, mmm?" This time he did take her elbow and led her toward the neon-lit exit.

"I can't just leave in the middle of my shift."

"Wanna bet?" He grabbed the tray from her hands, passed it to a waitress walking by and winked his thanks. Shrugging from his jacket, he draped it across Ellie's shoulders and guided her through the mass of gyrating bodies.

"Hey, baby doll, how 'bout another number?" Someone called to her.

"Later." Ellie waved. "Taking a break."

"Cutest singin' cocktail—"

"Trot on over, babe." Raucous laughter.

A man staggered toward her and a camera flashed. Peter swung his arm out and knocked the camera from the snapper, sending it crashing to the floor. Shoving a hand in his pocket, he pulled out a couple of hundred-dollar bills and hurled them on the floor. "That should cover the damages, Louie," he bit out, his eyes hard.

The loud music had muted the altercation and no one seemed to have noticed, except the three of them.

"What's going on?" Ellie glared at Peter, then turned to the barrel-shaped man pocketing the cash and scuttling across the floor for his camera.

Taciturn, Peter wove his way through the throng and pulled her with him.

"We can do publicity shots tomorrow, Louie," Ellie called over her shoulder.

"Sure thing, sugar."

The familiarity of his words made Peter pause mid-stride. He flexed his hand in a fist, thought better of it, and marched her away from the crowd.

"What're you doing?" She stopped, forcing him to turn around.

"Taking you home."

"You have no right—"

4

"I have every right … wife."

"Don't call me—"

Murderous silence.

"Technically, I guess I am."

Peter tightened his fingers on her arm. When she whimpered, he loosened his hold, but didn't release her. Smoke and alcohol clung to her, but a hint of her perfume reached him, making him ache for her. She'd just kicked him in the teeth, nearly denying their relationship as husband and wife. He steeled his jaw. When he was done with her, he'd boot her out. His eyes narrowed. He'd get what he wanted, including answers to questions that had battered his brain for the last three months. He had a right to know why she had left him. And at this crucial time. Why she preferred to live like a pauper, instead of like a princess with him? Why?

Dragging her with him, he climbed the four steps from the Hollywood cellar club to street level. Behind them, the neon sign flashed, *The Blue Room*, both illuminating and shading her face.

"Let go, Peter." She yanked her hand from his grasp and he allowed it. "I'm not about to run away at this time of night and in this weather." She drew the lapels of his jacket closer about her neck, raindrops drenching her hair and trickling down her nape.

"Stand under the canopy, Ellie," he commanded. "I'll wave down a cab."

From beneath her lashes, she watched him, studying him, loving him, hating—abruptly she froze, her thoughts ripping her apart. She'd wanted for nothing. He always brought her things, even during their most intimate moments. Heat infused her body and a drop of moisture slid between her breasts. All the material wealth he showered upon her couldn't make up for the limiting lifestyle as the wealthy Italian's wife, which made her feel more like his mistress.

She licked rain from her lips and her heart thudded. Was her husband an opportunist or simply too busy gaining wealth and power to notice her; to care that she had a dream of her own … wanted to make something of her own life?

He pushed a damp lock off his forehead with an impatient hand and stepped onto the sidewalk. He stretched out his arm to flag down a taxi, and his muscles contracted beneath his wet shirt.

Every cell of her body flared. She could easily succumb to his potent sexuality. But she had to resist the temptation. Had to resist his influence, his magnetism … him. A one-night stand with her husband would only compound the problem. Still vulnerable, she had to put distance between them, to think clearly; about their marriage, their life. Could they have a future together? She doubted it and her heart shriveled.

She drew in a breath, willed her erratic pulse to get in sync, and exhaled in a rush. Odor from the trash bins in the alley assailed the damp air, but she barely noticed. She took a step closer to him and reached out to touch him, to wrap her arms around the bulge of his biceps, to rub her cheek … feeling his strength. His security. His love.

Oh, how she wanted to, but instead she dropped her hand to her side and stepped back. She blinked raindrops from her lashes. It couldn't be as she wanted. A gust of wind silenced the cry from her lips. To be with him, she'd have to 'sell out' on herself; for chasing her dream could cost him his.

Entry level into the music biz entailed gigs in questionable locales and servicing all manner of clientele. It was a highly unsuitable vocation for the wife of the ambitious intern seeking a seat on the Medical Board.

Goosebumps erupted all over her skin. Yet, his ruthless climb to fame on the global front had strangled her dream. Stifled her.

She felt cornered.
Defeated.

That's why she'd left. Guilt gnawed her insides. Why she must slip away from him again.

Peter whistled and waved down an approaching cab. When the car screeched to a halt at the curb, tires splashing muddied water everywhere, she disappeared into the shadows of the night.

Chapter 2

He was losing his mind. He tossed and turned on the sofa in the living room of his Beverly Hills mansion. Where had she gone? Last night, he hailed the cab and glanced behind him for Ellie, but she'd vanished again. Taking his heart, his hopes, and his future with her. He hunted for her everywhere, questioned everyone in the club, and then he spotted the paparazzo at the bar. He shoved his way through the crowded room, grabbed Louie by the shirt collar and hauled him off the stool, his feet dangling in midair.

The man shook his head, his eyes nearly popping out of their sockets.

A camera flashed.

Disgusted, Peter dropped him on his feet and stomped back out to the street, the drizzle of rain cooling his skin. He asked everyone in the vicinity – the newsvendor on the corner, the laughing couple stepping out of the nearby pizzeria, the homeless person rifling through the trash cans in the alley, the waiting taxi driver.

No one had seen her.

Dawn was breaking by the time Peter had stumbled up the front steps of his home. He slammed the door shut and the sound echoed the emptiness of his life since she'd fled. After loosening his tie, he'd thrown himself on the living-room couch, the silence of the mansion deafening.

Now, he stared at the ceiling, his bloodshot eyes stinging from his sleepless night. How could she slip away with him not two feet from her? He flung an arm across his eyes. How could she leave him without an explanation? Not once, not twice, but thrice.

Shifting, he peered at the clock above the marble mantel of the fireplace. He groaned. Seven a.m. He glanced at his wrinkled, mud-stained clothes in distaste and scrubbed a hand across his stubble-ridden jaw. Time he took a shower and changed. He made to get up, but every muscle in his body resisted.

He slumped back on the cushions, and a self-deprecating smile cracked his mouth. As the doctor in the house, he certainly did not give himself sound advice. A highly esteemed neurosurgeon, who could heal all manner of ills of the human brain, yet he didn't know what to prescribe for a shattered heart.

A growl tore from him, ripping across the silent house. He lowered his lashes, cushioning his pupils, and swung his legs over the side of the couch. The movement shot sharp arrows through him, and his muscles contracted. He pinched the bridge of his nose and rolled his shoulders to get the blood circulating.

All night, he'd been coiled like a spring, ready to snap. He still had no inkling why his wife of five years had up and deserted him. Ungrateful little bi—but the voice in his head eclipsed that unsavory thought. *You were hardly around … itself a form of abandonment.*

He snorted. "What I've done, I've done for her." His chin jutted in defense. "Gave her a beautiful home, a new car every year, everything money could buy." The niggle in his head persisted. *That's not what she needed.* "What was it she needed?" His words exploded against the walls, adorned with priceless paintings. "What did she want?" Obviously, it hadn't been him.

9

The hole in his gut ached. He clutched his head between his hands, his temples pounding. A raw gash in his heart had split open and spurted blood … Ellie was the only one who could stop the hemorrhage. A menacing sound gurgled in his throat. She defied him by deftly slipping away from him – three times. That thrust the knife deeper into his aorta and proved she wasn't interested in handing him a band-aid.

He had no choice but to play hardball … with her.

There was too much at stake … his life, his profession, and his reputation. Then there were others—

The sudden ringing of the telephone had him almost jumping from his skin. He thought to ignore it, but the sound penetrated through the fog of his mind, his pain, and his fury. With every muscle throbbing, he reached for the cordless phone on the coffee table. Cherry red. *Her favorite color.* "Shut up," he muttered to the noise in his head.

He heaved a deep breath and exhaled with force. "He-l-lo," he croaked, then cleared his throat. "Hello."

* * *

"Three dollars." Ellie clutched the money in her hand and glanced at her empty wallet. Then she rifled through the bills, fingers shaking, to ensure she had counted correctly. She had.

She leaned against the sooty wall of the matchbox she'd called home for the last three months and closed her eyes. No money. No job. No prospects. She balled her hand into a fist and pressed it against her mouth, swallowing desperation. "I will not go back to him like I did at Christmas."

The sound of her breathing vibrated around her. She shoved the wallet back in her purse, slipped the strap over her shoulder and glanced about. Faded curtains hung on the one window, not quite blocking the sound of rain shooting against the pane. Wind whistled through the maple branches scraping against the

10

building, cars honked, and tires swished on wet roads of down-town North Hollywood.

She drew the lapels of her brown coat under her chin, her eyes following the crack in the wall from the stove to the stained sink and to the refrigerator. Shifting, her gaze settled on the frayed sofa that doubled as her bed; the blotchy dandelion hue matched the carpet. What a color scheme, she mused, the tight line across her mouth twitching, but not quite making it to a smile. The nearby table held her one luxury. A cell phone. Cherry red.

She glanced outside at shops still decorated with cupids and hearts, and her eyes filled with tears. Heaving a tremulous breath, she blinked them away, and her thoughts drifted back to her former life. It had included a luxurious Beverly Hills estate, a beachfront penthouse on the Italian Riviera, chauffeur-driven limos, servants ... gowns, jewelry ... money ... and a husband who was virtually a stranger. Pain and disillusionment mocked her; yet, beneath it all another feeling persisted.

She bit her lip, knowing she couldn't give into it. If she returned to him now, without anything resolved between them, it'd be business as usual with the sexy doctor.

With determined effort, Ellie severed her thoughts from the past and glanced in the mirror behind the door. She combed her fingers through her hair, scooped it up, and tucked it beneath a wool cap. Pinching her cheeks to add color, she took a deep breath and reached for the doorknob. At that moment, the doorbell rang and made her jump. She pulled the door open and her vitals went into overdrive.

"Go away." She forced the words between her stiff lips.

"No."

"What do you want?" She twisted the purse strap around her fingers.

"Answers."

Peter towered above her, his six-foot frame hidden beneath an Armani overcoat, his hair damp from rain. She wanted to run to him, yet she'd run away from him, three times. Not proud of it. But she'd been desperate to crack through his professional veneer, willing him to see *her* and not what she represented – a necessity for his next promotion.

"I-I have nothing more to say to you." She squeezed the doorknob, its metal ridges pressing into her palm.

He took a step closer.

She nudged the door closed, but he blocked it with his shoulder.

"Nonsense, Ellie." Flecks in his eyes turned coal black and he stepped inside, booting the door shut with his heel. "I deserve an explanation. Demand it."

"Explanation?" She moved two paces back and a sound, almost a snort, burst from her mouth. "You mean, like in talk?"

A perplexed look skimmed across his face.

"You never listened. Or weren't there. Or it wasn't the right time. Too tired. And most often you just wanted to … uh …"

"Yes?"

A blush warmed her cheeks.

"And was that so bad?" He brushed the color on her cheek with his knuckles. "To love you?" His words were so gentle that she almost crumbled in her resolve.

"No … yes … I mean no, but—"

Peter flicked his eyes across her agitated breasts, then lower, pausing at the apex of her thighs. A tense beat, and he glanced back up, clashing with her mutinous face.

"Don't provoke me, Peter." She yanked the hat lower over her ears.

"What's the matter?" He stepped closer, and she smelled the damp wool of his coat. His rain-fresh scent was intoxicating … putting her senses on full alert. "Afraid you might still feel something for me?"

She snapped out of the sexual trance. "The only thing I feel for you i-is indifference." *Not true*, the voice in her head jabbed. Be quiet!

He blanched, his proud features more pronounced. "I could prove otherwise." His warm breath teased the curls springing loose from the confines of her hat and sensitized her skin with awareness.

"Why are you here, Peter?" She walked backward until her legs bumped the sofa. "Besides trying to force yourself upon me."

A loaded moment, and she glimpsed something in his eyes ... pain?

She doubted if he could feel anything but arrogance. Nevertheless, she knew her words weren't quite fair.

"I have never forced—"

"I know." She sighed, glancing down at her scruffy boots. "I-I'm sorry. I didn't mean that."

He rubbed his forehead with his fingers and his wedding ring glinted in the dim light. The motion mesmerized her. She remembered holding his hand, feeling his strength, kissing, tasting, wanted to ... no!

"How'd you find me at the club?" she blurted,

His eyes glittered with purpose, his cheekbones prominent. "A friend tipped me off—"

"A spy."

"Hardly that, Ellie." An unbidden smile tugged at his lips. "A patron at the club—"

"I was fired this morning."

"Oh?" He flicked a speck of imaginary lint off his sleeve. "Rather sudden, wasn't it?"

She narrowed her eyes. "Yes, it was." She bet he had something to do with it. Her throat constricted. He had everything to do with it.

"You can't want to stay in this place."

"Why not?"

He raised a thick eyebrow.

"Not up to your level?"

"No," he growled. "Nor yours."

She laughed and the brittle sound bounced off grease-spattered walls. "Peter, you don't know that."

He brushed her shoulder. "Have you changed so quickly?"

"No." She closed her hands tight. "It took me five years."

During which time her life had revolved around a series of society events, elaborate luncheons, and schmoozing parties. Whenever Peter showed her off for the cameras, she wondered if he wanted her or the image of 'the good doctor's wife'. An appearance that was necessary for building his image as the successful neurosurgeon at the top of his game on the home front and on a global scale.

"Explain that ridiculous remark." He shuttered his eyes, sizing her up.

"Never mind." She sank on the sofa, before her legs buckled beneath her, and folded her hands in her lap.

"I do mind, Ellie."

"Why?"

"This is a dump," he bit out. "No wife of mine's going to be seen—"

"I knew it." She leaped to her feet. "You're more concerned about what other people think than what I think. Feel. Want."

"Not true."

"How's that?"

"Would I be here, otherwise?"

"Yes." She shot him a sharp gaze. "If it served your agenda."

His eyes darkened, reminding her of a raging bull. "What's my agenda, Ellie?"

"To reach the top at any cost."

"Because?"

"We-ell … uh … uh …" She blinked, at a loss for words.

"Not sure?"

Had she misjudged him?

"Did it ever occur to you that I work hard to provide a good home for you, us?"

"A showplace—"

"So you can have everything you want—"

"Despise."

"Do you?"

"Ye-es."

Peter slitted his focus and camouflaged the inferno inside him. Her words were barbs in his flesh, but her body heat, hinting of roses, wrapped around him like a caress. He'd tasted her, had her, and would again. His groin tightened, breath billowed in his chest, and his heart thudded. He was losing the fight of his life, with the most important person in his life.

His wife.

He sensed it in his gut and something seemed to die inside him. Anger flared through him and eclipsed the ache scraping him raw.

"Then there's nothing more to say, except—" He bridged the gap between them in one stride, his legs brushing her thighs, "—this." He hauled her hard against his chest, his gaze connecting with hers for a timeless second, and then, he imprisoned her mouth with his.

Ellie wriggled in his embrace, but his lips were a sensual delight, evoking a response from her. As always. When his tongue slid into her mouth, awakening every cell, she curved into his embrace, and kissed him back full force. She reached up to wrap her arms around his neck and her purse swung out, knocking the telephone off the table.

The sound penetrated their heat and she pulled away. "N-o-o, please."

"You could've fooled me." His words heavy, his breath fanning her mouth. But he let her go.

"That's all I am to you." She stumbled back a step and grabbed onto the sofa. "Someone to warm your bed and satisfy your basic needs."

"If that's all you were," he muttered, swallowing deep puffs of air, "I wouldn't have married you."

"Why did you?" Her words were so soft; he had to strain to hear.

"You need to ask?" He met and held her gaze for the longest moment. When she didn't answer, he walked to the window and propped his hip against the ledge. "Ellie, you can't mean to live here. You have no money, no job—"

"You made sure of that."

He scrubbed his cheek with the back of his hand. A man in his position had connections. He used them. He refused to feel guilty. He wanted what was best for her. *And for yours truly*, the taunt stabbed. He dismissed it. Working in that seedy nightclub was not for this woman, who'd taken his name and became a part of his soul. Every muscle of his torso tightened. She behaved like he was the enemy. "You have no prospects."

She started to laugh. A soft sound at first, then it grew to a high pitch.

"What's the matter?" He made to grab her, changed his mind, and stuffed his hands in his coat pockets.

She swallowed and the sound muted. "Nothing. Everyth—"

"Then, come home."

"I have no *home*, Peter."

"No?"

She remained silent.

He winced.

The sound of their breathing compounded the awkward moment.

He reached out to touch her hair, and then checked the motion. "Accept the credit cards – to pay rent, food—"

"No," she fired back. "I want nothing from you. I want to be free."

A lacerated sound burst from his mouth. He'd grown up in a household of near-starving kids while his mother sewed into the early hours of the morning, then cleaned houses to help feed and clothe them. To keep a roof over their heads, his father, an immigrant, speaking broken English, worked in kitchens with soap suds to his elbows while the affluent in society dined out.

Peter had cringed with embarrassment every time someone mispronounced his name and wished he could fit in better. Of course, he never had. So, from an early age, he hit the streets of Little Italy in New York, vowing to opt out of that life, make something of himself, help his family have a better life, and aid others in need. Never having to go to sleep clutching his growling stomach. Never to feel the stigma of being a foreigner and wearing hand-me-downs from well-meaning neighbors. Never to have others look at him with pity because of his background or the sound of his name.

"You think living like a pauper is going to make you free?" he said, his words a growl.

"Of you," she fired back, her words a stake in his heart.

He nearly doubled over. "Think again, hard."

She dropped down on the sofa and adjusted the cap over her ears.

"Don't glamorize poverty," he said, his tone curt. "You don't want to do poor, Ellie."

"I'd rather be poor and free, than like … like Rapunzel in her tower."

"Do you realize what you're saying?"

"Ye-es," she said, her eyes sparking fire. "I'd rather be poor and happy than—"

"And how many poor happy people do you know?" he asked, his words cynical.

"I haven't counted—"

He guffawed, a dry, humorless sound, and eclipsed her flip retort.

"Money, power, and prestige are the only things that matter to you," she said, tone resigned.

"Where did you get that idea?"

"From what you've done."

"What's that?"

"You've put your profession before our marriage a-and everything."

"And that makes me a bad guy?"

"I don't know." She crinkled her forehead. "I thought—"

"You thought wrong." He paced the floor twice. "There's a great deal you don't know about me, *amore mia*."

"Why's that?"

He shrugged.

She frisked him with her eyes. "You're a real smooth operator." A smile teased the corner of her mouth, and she nipped it away with her teeth. "Didn't mean it to come out a pun."

He cocked his head, debated, and then simply said, "You could be mistaken in your assessment."

His childhood hadn't seemed to matter, so he hadn't told her. Later, he'd gotten buried in work and when he surfaced, he wanted to hold her, love her. Apparently, that hadn't been enough for her.

He rubbed the back of his neck and refrained from confiding in her, still. Maybe he wanted her to take him at face value. Wanted her to think more of him than the shallow, controlling bastard she coined him.

"It doesn't matter," she said.

"No?"

"No, yes." She avoided meeting his searching gaze. "I don't know."

He was silent for a long moment, and then nodded. "How will you live? What will you do?"

"I'll sing for my supper," she tossed back.

"Parading yourself before—"

She leaped up, but he grabbed her arm before she found her mark. Her gaze collided with his midnight-blues. Her chest heaved. His nostrils flared. The silent war waged between them, then she twisted from his grasp,rubbing her wrist.

"Did I hurt—?" He reached for her.

"No." She half-turned from him, knowing in her heart this man would never, could never, hurt her. Then why was she putting them through purgatory? Her heart bled. Because she preferred to go through it than dwell on it. "I-I'll be fine."

"You can't make a decent living without some skill."

"I'll learn." She stood erect to her full five-foot four inches, not wanting him to dwarf her.

"Everything's high tech."

"I'll take a class."

"Costs money."

"I have—" He lifted an eyebrow, and she amended, "I'll find work in one of the clu ... er ... restaurants."

He set his mouth, not missing her near slip, but chose not to address it. "In the meantime?"

"I'll manage."

"How?"

Exasperated at his inquisition, she blurted, "I'll marry money."

He laughed, a savage sound. "You're married to money now." Silence thickened, tension built and crackled with his flint-hard words.

"Admit it, Ellie." He curled his lip, contempt carving his features. "You didn't marry me. You married my pocketbook."

"No." She reached for him, but when he twisted away, she glanced down at her boots. She hadn't meant those harsh words. Said them to annoy him, because she hurt being so close to him and him not understanding her. She peeked at him through her lashes, but the wall of his back pricked her resentment.

It had always been about his life, his career, and his agenda. While he flourished, she wasted away. But Ellie could no longer deny herself. Not for her parents. Not for her husband. She had to take a firm stand to show him, and herself, that she was more than the millionaire doctor's appendage.

"Why did you marry me, Ellie?" He spun around, snaring her in his hypnotic gaze. "If not for cash to anchor papa—"

Her eyes snapped open wide. "Don't you dare drag him into this."

But fury fueled him, and he was on the attack. "—drowning in the bottle … getting sacked ag—"

"I won't hear you bad-mouthing—"

He tossed his head back and laughed, the sound sending chills chasing up her spine.

"He's working at the University of Sussex … he's keeping it together … taking care of mom and Joey," she said, feeling the need to defend him. "He's in rehab."

"So he is." Peter stroked his chin deep in thought. "Took long enough to get him there."

"What's that supposed to mean?"

He shrugged.

"They're doing okay." She raised her chin to score her point and glanced away from his laser-sharp look.

Wind-tossed rain slashed against the windowpane, compounding the bleakness of her mood. Her shoulders sagged.

"Good to hear," Peter said, his words clipped. "But for how long?"

"You wouldn't dare eclipse his job like you did mine."

A dangerous pause, and his eyes glinted like agates.

"My net worth had nothing to do with us?" he ground out, her accusation nicking his pride.

"Everything isn't about dollars and cents."

"No?" His lip curled with cynicism. "You said 'I do' because …" he prompted.

"Oh, you're impossible," she fired back and fell into the ocean storm of his eyes. Confused, she blinked. "Same reason you married me."

"That is?" He held her gaze captive.

"I-I-I …" She inched away from him, clutching the seams of her coat. "Peter, I—"

"Let's find out, shall we?"

"Wha-at do you mean?"

He brushed his thumb across her bottom lip. "Good-bye, Ellie."

Chapter 3

The slamming of the front door echoed in her ears, and she collapsed on the sofa. "Goo-ood-bye, Peter."

It was what she wanted, after all. For him to be away from her, so she could think straight and get her life in order. But why was her heart splintering and her breath gagging in her throat? She squeezed her hands closed and her fingernails dug into her palms. *Be strong.* She burst into tears, the past flitting through her mind for what seemed like an eternity.

A heavy sigh resonated from deep inside her and she swiped at her cheeks. She had to get something to eat. How far could she stretch three dollars? Even a McDonald's burger and fries spun into the stratosphere.

A wistful smile brushed her mouth. She tried to push herself up, but her lethargic body resisted. She fell back on the cushions. Despair filled her. She gave in and closed her eyes … just for a minute.

Time ticked by.

She couldn't stay here. The walls seemed to be closing in around her. Memories haunted, taunted her. She dragged herself up and the room swayed every which way. She groaned and clutched her temples.

Disorientated, she burst through the front door and dashed down the dimly lit stairs. In her haste, she tripped over the third step and hurled headlong down to the landing, her scream muted by blaring horns of rush-hour traffic. Blackness sucked her under.

* * *

Dr. Peter Medeci heard the ambulance siren and hurried to the Emergency of St. Joseph's Hospital. Two medics were rushing in with the injured on a stretcher.

"911 call," one said, while a third handed him the report. "Caucasian female, twenty-eight, head trauma."

Peter glanced at the chart and shifted his gaze to the patient. His vitals short-circuited. Blood drained from his face, and he struggled for oxygen, his heart seeming to freeze in his chest. Then, his years of professional discipline kicked in. He pressed his fingers at the pulse point of her wrist and sent up a prayer of thanks. The gash on her forehead, he didn't like.

"X-rays!" he barked, his pulse pummeling a hole in his chest. He hurried along beside the gurney, holding Ellie's hand all the way.

When he had to relinquish her into another doctor's care, he nearly exploded. But he insisted on spending the night by her side and slouched in the visitor's chair, he challenged anyone who even tried to oust him.

In the morning, Peter dragged himself away to take a quick shower, change his clothes, and check on his own patients.

At eight a.m. he strode into Ellie's room, carrying a bouquet of red roses he'd bought from the shop in the hospital lobby. "What the—?" His mind rejected the evidence of the empty bed. No. She couldn't have left without someone seeing her. Not from here. He heard the running water in the adjoining bathroom and relief ripped through him. He plunked down in the chair in the corner and waited.

The door clicked open and tension eased from his shoulders. "How are you feeling—?" he asked, words getting blocked in his throat.

She'd changed back into the torn dress they brought her in. Her golden-brown curls had been swept off her brow, making room for the gauze bandage that almost matched the paleness of her skin. Her pupils were still dilated, the fawn-brown of her irises too bright.

"Good morning, Peter." She wrinkled her pert nose at the medicinal smells in the room and scrubbed a dirt stain on her sleeve.

"That won't get it clean." He offered her the roses.

She hesitated and then took them in her hands, breathing their scent. When she glanced at him over the blooms, their eyes clashed, and a jolt charged through him. Memories whizzed by, time stood suspended.

She blinked and the moment shattered. "I-I'm fine, thank you."

He squinted, his gaze laser-sharp. Her words were a little too emotionless, a little too impersonal. Could it be the effect of the clinical atmosphere, or, and his heart clubbed his chest, a reflection of what their relationship was to be? Over?

"Good."

Setting the flowers on the bedside table, she snatched up her coat from the closet, draped it over her arm and rifled for something in her purse. He curved his mouth into a half-smile when she found it. She glanced into the mirror above the sink and outlined her lips. Cherry red.

"Nice."

"Thanks."

He clenched his belly, remembering the sweet taste of her lips, the feel of her silky skin ... her breasts fit so perfectly in his hands, her nipples hardening in his mouth ... He nearly groaned aloud, but shoved the sound back down his throat. *Get a grip, Doc.*

A myriad of emotions—anger, wistfulness, desire, hurt, pride, disillusionment, and exasperation churned inside him. "Going somewhere?" he asked, feigning indifference.

"Home."

"Good." Adjusting the stethoscope around his neck, he rose from the chair. "I'm off in half an hour. I'll drive us home."

A silent moment, and she turned, not quite meeting his eyes. "I'll be going home alone."

"Okay. I'll meet you there, later." He was clutching at straws.

"No." She squeezed the lipstick between her fingers.

Good thing she replaced the top or she'd have cherry flavoring spurting all over her palm. He'd have to lick it clean, tasting her ... *basta*!

A grown man ... a smitten Doc ... a fool?

He shook his head, dismissing the vexing thought. She dropped the lipstick in her purse, clicked it closed and the bag slipped from her fingers.

"I got it, Ellie." Peter bent to retrieve it, but she swept it up in her hand. When she made to stand, she shut her eyes and reached out for anything, anyone for support.

"Woman, why—" Peter lifted her up in his arms, his heartbeat catapulting into hers, and placed her on the bed. Taking her wrist, he pressed his fingers on her flesh and checked her pulse. "You must relax, Ellie."

She cast him a look, like his medical advice came from outer space. "I don't have time."

"Make time."

"I have to work—"

"You don't—"

"Or I'll be evicted from my apartment."

"So?"

"No."

He nodded. "You must rest." A plan was formulating in his brain. "Even a mild concussion can rear its ugly head. Migraine, dizziness."

"I'll be fine."

"Of course." A deep pause. "In about three weeks."

She'd torn his male pride to shreds.

"I can't."

"You can."

His ego was shattered.

His wife, whom he showered with gifts, treated like a princess and who shared the most intimate moments of his life … blood flooded his male parts, pulsing heat. She couldn't wait to bail out even in her injured state. Why was that? He sucked in a mouthful of air and it seethed out between his teeth. What was she hiding?

His belly turned to lead, his heart to stone.

The time had come to teach her a lesson that'd have her crawling back to him. He set his mouth in a harsh line. Then it'd be, *arrivederci,* babe.

"What do you mean?" she asked.

"You seem to want to end our marriage so—" He sat on the corner of the bed, the mattress depressing beneath his weight. "I'll play your game."

"I'm not playing games, Peter."

"By my rules."

"It's always by your rules."

He allowed her comment to whiz by and tilted his head, his tone cool.

"I'll give you a divorce, Ellie."

She blanched. "Di-divorce?"

He steeled his jaw and the Roman warrior booted up. "On one condition."

Suspicion tinted her eyes a darker shade of brown. "Go on."

Relief raced through him. At least she hadn't said no. "We live together as husband and wife for the next three weeks." He determined to have her, take her one more time, and get her out of his system.

"Why three weeks?"

"Mild as your injury is, it'll take you about that long to recuperate." He adjusted the collar of his lab coat, ignoring the jab to his conscience.

"You can't live in that dingy flat on your own in this condition."

"Guilty?"

"Naaa," he said, tone nonchalant. "Sensible."

"Of course." And she was anything but sensible, was what he thought. Why else would she opt to play the clubs when she had Prince Charming in hand? But did she really? Ellie squinted up at him, her intuition prickling her insides. He was up to something. "I could stay with my parents."

"You could." He brushed his chin with the back of his hand. "The long flight to London wouldn't be advisable." He cast her a steady gaze.

"And I know you don't want to worry them and your little bro—"

"He's not so little anymore."

"What's he … six … seven?"

"He's eight years old, plays soccer … er … football to the Brits and—"

"Okay, dully censured." A rueful smile brushed across his mouth.

"Do you blame me?" Her brother had been three when Peter met him for the first and only time, at their wedding. When Ellie visited her family, Peter sent gifts, but stayed behind working the emergency shift.

"No blame, Ellie. Priority."

"Obviously, your priorities differ from mine."

"We'll know soon enough."

"What d' you mean?" She wriggled to a sitting position and he adjusted the pillows behind her head. He smelled fresh … of soap … his hair still damp from his shower. She wanted to—she

27

gulped down the whimper rising in her throat.

"At the end of three weeks, you'll have what you want," he said.

"Will I?" she asked, her gaze searching. "Will you?"

He inclined his head, his eyes piercing blue cobalt. "I'll make sure of it."

His arrogant words bore a hole into her, his gaze searing her icy skin. He'd thrown down the gauntlet and she'd picked it up, or more accurately, she'd hurled it at him by leaving, and he'd caught it.

"What if I refuse?"

A telling pause.

"I wouldn't recommend it."

She squinted her eyes at him, her hand fluttering to her throat. "What's that supposed to mean?"

He slapped his ace in her face. "If the university regents get a whiff of papa's philandering with the bottle on the side …" he let his words trail off, his meaning unmistakable.

"You wouldn't stoop so low—"

"Try me, *mia esposa*," he muttered, his words flint-hard, his eyes glacial.

She blinked her lashes to stay the tears. Just last week, her mom had moaned into the phone about grocery prices, mortgage rates rising, and fuel costs hitting record highs. If her father backslid on the booze and lost this job, they'd be in the gutter.

It had taken Ellie some time to calm her mother's fears and her own. But with the photo shoot Louie had lined up and the singing gigs in *The Blue Room*, she'd make enough to help them without going to Peter like a beggar maid. She squirmed at that unpalatable image.

Finally, she thought she'd gotten a handle on her life and could do something for herself; show Peter that if he wanted their marriage to work, he'd have to make some major changes. But it had blown up in her face.

A sound like a muted wail burst from her, and had him studying her through his narrow focus.

Once again, Peter called the shots, and she ducked. Her spirit rebelled at his high-handedness, at the unfairness, at feeling powerless. Then, a glimmer of female intuition had her mouth curving a smile. Not totally powerless. She had her own card to play.

"Ex *sposa*."

He shrugged. "In three weeks."

His indifference stoked her already frazzled emotions. She wanted to lash out at him; vent her frustration, hurt, anger, hurl her purse at him, stomp her feet, scream. But it wouldn't do. He'd surmise it was reaction from her head injury. Cool, calm, and collected was a better way to go … a persona she perfected over the years as the good *dottore's* wife. It'd hold her in good stead, until she waved, s' long buster.

But first, she'd dish up a dose of the doctor's own medicine and have him groveling at her feet. "Uncontested?"

He drilled her with his midnight-hard gaze. "Yes." He coughed, smothering the word with the back of his hand.

Divorce. Such an ugly word and it carried an even uglier feeling with it. Her heart plummeted. He not only called her bluff and managed to hand-cuff her to him again, but had the situation already resolved post three weeks. Why the delay? He might want to appease his conscience due to her injury, but instinct told her it had to do with more than that.

Much more.

So be it. No talk, just action. Hard, cold decisions. Something she was fast learning from her renegade Doc, as some decked him. She ignored the stab to her heart. It was time to match him. "Agreed." Her gaze level with his. "Except—"

"Yes?" He was studying every nuance of emotion fleeting across her features, and his intense scrutiny had her nerves twitching.

"I want to keep my apartment in North Hollywood." She might be out of a marriage in three weeks, but she refused to be homeless into the bargain. Of course, Peter wouldn't permit that. He'd feel obligated … she'd feel like a kept woman. She tightened her fingers over her handbag; her sense of self-worth could no longer allow that.

Who was Ellie Ross Medeci, besides the good doctor's wife? Must she always defer to him? Her dream of being a recording artist had been shattered twice over.

First, when the responsibility for her family's finances fell on her shoulders, she opted for a less-risky study choice, fashion design and marketing. But when cash pared down to the wire, she had to let that go too, and work the library day shift. That, together with moonlighting at the local pub, brought in a decent wage that kept them in a house.

Second, when she married Peter and was expected to behave with a certain sense of decorum as his wife. Which in itself had been far more restrictive, sucking life from her. Did he even know, care? Or would he see her rekindled passion for her own aspirations as a cheap shot to undermine his, even after she'd shelved them for five years?

She sighed. It didn't matter now, for her well-laid plans had hit the dust. Seemed he was using her escapade as an excuse to unload her. She curled her fingers into fists, and her American grit kicked in. Knowing that shoebox of an apartment was hers gave her a sense of security.

"Why?" he asked.

She shrugged and a sliver of satisfaction rippled through her. At least he was still curious enough to ask. Ammo she might use in the future?

"Not thinking of running away before three weeks are you?" he said. "Three times' the charm, so I hear."

She fiddled with the button on her coat, not missing the mockery in his tone. She had already run out on him thrice, after all. "No."

He studied her beneath his furrowed brows. "Very well."

"And ..." Her stomach dipped, her palms moist, but she forced the words out. "I-I'll not sleep with you."

His eyes darkened. Then, he chuckled. "Afraid?"

"No." She could play cat and mouse too. "You did say it would take some time for me to recover" – she brushed her fingers across her bandaged brow – "and with headaches coming on ..." She allowed her words to trail away and watched him from the corner of her eye.

A pause then, "Done."

Disappointment washed over her. He agreed so quickly. At the least, she hoped, she'd have to convince him. But no. Dr. Medeci knew his mind, knew what he wanted, and got it. She wondered if she imagined his heart beating in time with her own anytime during the last five years.

"Go-ood." The word stumbled from her mouth.

Was it? Peter doubted it. Dangerous would be how he'd dub it. His personal and professional lives were pitted against each other and about to detonate. When he caught the look of consternation on her face, he almost retracted his cruel words. But then, her brittle words smacked him in the solar plexus, a reminder he could lose all. He couldn't afford going soft on her. His next move had to be right on target ... too many others would be slammed if he didn't coup the Chairmanship of the Medical Board.

A nerve battered his cheek with brutal force.

He thrived on the edge on a daily basis, but hadn't thought he'd have to tread the high wire with Ellie too. He drew air into his lungs; it expanded and burst from his mouth in a violent sound. Had the sweet, loving girl he married been an illusion? Had *they* gotten to her? Would she topple his political plans?

He gulped down the bitter taste scarring his throat. He had to know.

"Will you be ready to leave in a few minutes?" He caught a speck of pain in her eyes, but she fluttered her lashes and it vanished. A trick of the light, he concluded.

Why put himself through this? Why not just send her packing now? Because he'd fought for everything he had in this life, including Ellie. And he didn't like to lose. If he had to give her up, then he'd do it his way, by his rules and in his own time.

"Have you anything else to take than what you're wearing?"

"No," she murmured.

A deadly silence.

He took something from his pocket and his whole body seemed to go rigid, the muscles in his neck cording. "This belongs on your finger." The gold band looped through a string of tiny beads nestled in his palm.

"I-I-I wore it around my neck." She snatched it from him, wondering if he recognized the necklace he'd bought for her from a street vendor on their first date. Even when she was decked in diamonds for some glam event, she wore it always. "Tips were better if customers thought I was—"

"Single?"

She nodded.

"We won't have that problem for the next three weeks, will we?"

Silent, she slipped the ring on her finger and dropped the necklace in her purse. Snapping it shut, she tapped the clasp with her forefinger.

Nervous? He doubted it. Most likely, thinking of her life post three-week interlude.

She glanced at the bouquet of roses lying on the bedside table. A heartbeat, a breath, then he took the spray and tossed it to her. She caught it against her heart, and his pulse galloped. When she brushed her lips across the petals, his temperature hiked, the girth of his sex mounting. He shifted to ease the ache, his lab coat hiding the evidence of his desire from her.

War raged inside him. He must be out of his mind. After the hell she put him through, he still wanted her, fantasized … But the way he figured it, he'd seduce her once more and break her spell over him. No longer bewitched by her. Afterward, he'd give her what she wanted—otherwise why ditch out on him, not once, not twice, but thrice?

If she wanted her freedom, he'd oblige. On his terms. His gut recoiled, but he ignored the warning. A muscle pounded his throat. She'd put him through hell on a grill. He was determined to score … on all counts.

"I-I'm ready to leave," she said, making no move to do so.

Why didn't she just walk out the door like she'd done three months ago? Because although Ellie Ross Medeci was making a bid for her independence, she was no fool. To be totally free, she had to know how she fared in this test of wills … in this last stand with her husband. Ensure she came out with enough ammo so he could never blackmail her again … how dare he attempt to use her father as a bargaining chip to get to her.

Brave words, Ellie, but it worked … for here you are.

"*Bene*," Peter muttered, a tight line slashed across his mouth.

Her heart battled her mind. She must be feeling the effects of her head injury—she was treading dangerous ground to agree to live with him for three weeks. Knowing full well that one touch from him and she'd be lost. But the way she figured it, she'd prove to him that she didn't need him. Emotionally, physically, or financially. She would not succumb to his sexual magnetism. Then, she'd give him what he wanted—otherwise, why mention the dreaded D word?

If he wanted his freedom, she'd go along with it. On her terms. Her pulse kicked back in protest, but she dismissed the warning. She studied him from beneath her lashes. He'd broken her heart. She'd walk away the winner.

Chapter 4

Peter drove through the gates of his … their … home, steered the Mercedes along the driveway and pulled up at the front of the house. Rose bushes of every kind surrounded the imposing structure. Ellie pressed the bouquet against her heart, remembering waking up on sunny mornings to rose-scented breeze ruffling the sheer curtains in their bedroom. A wobbly breath and she smelled freshly mowed grass and honeysuckle, which meandered along the wrought-iron fence. It bordered several acres of land, including the gardener's cottage in back.

"Welcome home, *Signora* Medeci." Peter cast her a perfunctory glance, slid out, and walked around to the passenger door to open it for her.

Already half way out when he offered his hand to assist her, she ignored his chivalrous gesture and slammed the door behind her.

She could not touch him. If she did, it would be her downfall. Ice. That's the only way she'd combat the sexual attraction sizzling at his nearness. "Er … thanks."

She followed him up the veranda steps to the front door. He was a man who walked with confidence, who commanded respect because he had earned it. She could not deny him that. What she could deny him was herself, her heart. *You'd be denying yourself, girl*, the voice in her head reprimanded. Go away, she said. She refused to live in his shadow any longer. "I can find my own way."

"Glad to hear you still remember the way." He inserted the key in the lock, his words laced with sarcasm.

"I sure do." She couldn't help baiting him. "The way in and the way out."

He caught her in the laser beam of his eyes. "You certainly do."

"Ye-es," she murmured, hugging the roses to her bosom.

She had to keep her distance; must not fall for his sex appeal. If she faltered in her resolve, she'd lose. She glanced at his taciturn features. Reaching him on another level now would be like trying to break through a brick wall. She'd already gotten one crack on the head from her earlier tumble. She wasn't eager for another.

"This is where you belong." He opened the door wide. "Not in that two-bit hole you've been living in."

She spun to give him a tart response and clutched her head, her knees buckling. "Ooh-o-o."

Peter scooped her up in his arms and the flowers fluttered to the floor. "Wrap your arms around my neck," he said, tone firm. "I won't bite."

Ellie blinked at the bright spots bopping before her eyes and did as he asked, hair at his nape cushioning her fingers. High voltage zapped into her, scrambling her pulse. He smelled of soap and fresh air. It'd be so easy to burrow into his neck, nibble her way to his ear, and across his jaw to his mouth. Pretend this Arctic front between them was a bad dream. Peter strode across the threshold to the living room and broke the spell by plunking her down on the couch.

"I'll get the luggage," his said, his words curt.

"Whose?"

He chuckled. "That's right. You left your things at your … er … place."

"I have plenty more here." She brushed a hand across her eyes, thankful that the dizziness was diminishing. "In the upstairs closet."

He cast her a covert glance. "In our bedroom."

"I'll ask Marta to help move them to the guestroom," she said. Silence. Long, tense, and cold.

"No."

"We made an agreement."

"After your sudden departure, I gave the staff an extended vacation." He walked to the circular bar in the corner. "Drink?" He glanced at her bandaged temple. "A soft beverage would be best."

Ellie waved her hand, no.

"Marta comes by every couple of weeks to clean, cook, and stock the freezer." He seized a bottle of sparkling water, twisted the cap off, saluted her, and took several gulps. "Jose keeps an eye on the lawns." After contemplating the contents in the bottle, he took a last swig and set it on the counter. "I'll move your things into the other room."

"That means we're alone."

"That bother you?"

"Of course not." But her heart bounced against her ribs.

"Make yourself at … er … home," Peter said, a wry twist to his lips. "I won't take long." A steady gaze, then he turned and took the stairs two at a time to the second floor.

"Home." The word feathered from her lips and she scooted off the sofa. Could this ever be her home? A grand house, yes. A home, she doubted it.

Yet, during her short stay here, she was glad Marta wouldn't be taking over so completely she'd be shooed from the kitchen.

Ellie had played the lady of leisure far too long. Lazing away hours at the pool, strolling the property, shopping online, and cruising Rodeo Drive for the latest fashion trends. Gucci, Prada, Channel. She'd become a regular fashionista frequenting the gym, spa, beauty salon—manicurist, pedicurist, hairstylist, beautician. On 'show' with Peter at some medical event or other, she had to be on top form.

Outwardly she'd been a knockout, but inwardly she'd been a mess. The lavish pampering serviced her body, but not her soul. A sliver of fear pierced her. Twisting around, she glanced at the grounds through the window spanning one whole wall. Power walks around the estate and puttering in her miniature vegetable garden were more her style. Since it was February, she'd have to forego the latter, but she could certainly do the former, followed by a quick dip in the pool.

A wistful smile flitted across her mouth. At first, she'd been thrilled to be the bride of the up-and-coming young surgeon. He was hot, sexy, and good looking ... and generous. He supplied her with every material thing she could ever want. He had her on his arm at every medical function imaginable. And she glowed. Lived his life. Lived for him. Eventually, the lifestyle that played like a fairy tale lost its enchantment and nearly demolished her, keeping her own dreams under lock and key.

Peter became more preoccupied with his profession. His stellar success in wielding the knife had placed him in high demand on a global scale. He jetted both to major capitals of the world and to minor locales.

At the start, Ellie had accompanied him, and while he was in session, she played tourist—alone. She strolled along the River Thames, hopped on a double-decker to Buckingham Palace, Tower of London, and Westminster Abbey when on British soil; she climbed the Acropolis to the Parthenon, day-cruised Mediterranean islands, and over-tipped the slick-talking cabbies in Athens. At that recollection, she almost giggled. Riding the rented scooter to the Arc de Triomphe, Champs Elysées, Eiffel Tower and, of course, the haute couture scene in Paris had been fun. And so it had gone with other cities, in other countries, on other continents.

A sigh built inside her and she expelled the heavy sound. At night, she waited for Peter in their extravagant hotel suite to return from his speaking engagements and other commitments. With his reputation on the rise, he garnered accolades that held him in good stead for political gain in the medical field. He climbed the ranks and soon after landed a seat on the Medical Board.

Sought after more than ever, Peter began doing double duty on the domestic and global fronts.

Ellie hadn't accompanied him as often. Instead, she busied herself with social activities befitting her station as his wife. Since their high-caliber lifestyle alienated most of her friends, she drifted to his circle. But nothing could fill the void inside her that only he could satisfy.

Rubbing her hands over her arms, Ellie wandered around the living room. She trailed her fingers over priceless *objets d'art*, from the bronze statue to the porcelain vase in the corner of the room. When Peter finally plodded home, he was exhausted and in no mood to talk. Just dropped into bed and hauled her with him.

As time crawled by, their beautiful Beverly Hills mansion morphed into a gilded cage for Ellie. Emotionally depleted, she turned into a shell of herself. The emptiness of her life had taken its toll. She had no recourse but to flee the 'palace'. It had broken her heart to leave him, but if she hadn't, she'd have no heart at all. A distressing moan vibrated from deep in her throat.

When she heard the sound of Peter bounding down the stairs, she reined in her thoughts. He crossed the foyer, paused, and then his footsteps drew closer. Her nerves bounced. She took several deep breaths to center herself, but when he walked in, her pulse leaped.

"Your room's ready." He bridged the distance between them and dropped the roses into her arms.

"Tha-anks." She brushed the bruised petals with her fingertips, the sweet scent still vibrant.

"Hungry?" he asked. "Marta's left tacos and spaghetti in the freezer."

"No, thanks," she murmured, her words a hush ebbing around them.

"Som'm the matter?" he asked, studying her through his dark lashes.

Ellie shook her head, her hair brushing her shoulders. Peter clamped his teeth. Not long ago, he buried his face in the silky softness, the scent of her shampoo a balm to his stressed body. A heavy sound shot from deep inside him, echoing awareness between them.

"Som'm the matter?" she asked, her gaze glued on his features.

He shook his head. "Naaa." Then, he feigned a chuckle. "I'm going to grab a sandwich and hit the books."

"Of course," she said, tone dry.

He was quiet for a long moment, and then brushed his hand across his forehead. "Mega bucks are flowing in from hospital benefactors—"

"That you mobilized."

He shrugged. "Won't do any good unless I nix the motion that's about to hit the floor in the boardroom."

She crinkled her brow, wondering what he meant.

"I've become a threat to the *status quo*."

"Nooo," she said, tongue in cheek.

His mouth hinted a grin, but it faded with his next words. "The Chair can veto my proposal for research in support of upgrading the parking structure."

"You can't be serious."

"Mmm." He paused, a heavy beat. "And he'll use any means at his disposal to take me out." He gave her a level look. "A breath of scandal, real or fabricated, could tip the scales in his favor."

She squinted at him. "You're making another political play."

"I'm going to bump him in this next round." He curled his lip. "And with veto power—"

"You'd have more control."

He nodded. "By securing the Chair I'd muzzle the hound and his lackeys." It would stall the power struggle between politicians whose main interest was maintaining the *status quo* for financial gain and physicians whose priority was preserving human life at any price. Especially, for those who couldn't afford it.

"When will you know?"

"In about three—"

"—weeks," she finished for him.

An endless moment, explosive in its intensity, crackled between them.

Ellie laughed, igniting the loaded atmosphere. "I'm the whiff of scandal—" Giggles bubbled from her, and she laughed so hard, tears streamed down her face. "—that could cost you the Chairmanship on the Medical Board." She juggled the blooms in her arms and swiped at her cheeks. "That's why you came after me … had me fired." She hiccupped. "Brought me here, containing me until after the election."

He shook his head. "That's not the only reason—"

"We must keep up appearances, mustn't we?" Her voice climbed an octave higher and cracked. "A chanteuse wife singing for tips at the local nightclub wouldn't be up to standard."

"It's not what you think."

But she was on a roll. Anger and resentment erupted from her. "My stint in the club would've cramped your style, costing you votes." She paused for breath, a whizzing sound between her lips. "Not quite fitting the VIP image of Dr. Peter Medeci. But once you nailed the Chairmanship—" She smothered a sob with her fist. "I'm gone."

"It's not that simple, Ellie," he bit out, grabbing her by the shoulders.

"Aha! You admit it."

"I admit nothing."

Ellie shook free from his hold, breath bursting from her. "Don't manhandle me."

"You got it."

"You don't want a wife" she hurled the roses at him; he caught them and that pricked her ire even more. "You want a mannequin who'll submit to your every demand, in and out of bed."

Deafening silence, like the aftermath of an exploding bomb.

His eyes glittered with suppressed anger, and he tossed his own grenade. "You must've liked it real fine to stick around for five long ones."

Blood drained from her face and she grabbed the banister for support. He almost retracted his brutal words, but refrained, allowing them to stand as a shield between them. Had to keep his hands off her, otherwise he'd prove his words by taking her right there on the floor on a bed of rose petals.

Every muscle in his body knotted. That's not how he planned this interlude. He didn't want her wrath, he wanted her ardor, her admission … her love.

"You-ou arrogant bast—"

He clicked his tongue in censure, but since that only seemed to hike her temper, he backtracked toward the kitchen. "I'll put these in water."

"Oooo!" Ellie threw her hands up, took aim, and fired, "What if I won't play?"

He paused, and a beguiling smile curved his lips but didn't touch his eyes. "Why, then, you'll have a hard time singing for your supper when you leave here."

She gave him such a look of loathing it would've shriveled a lesser man. With head held high, she sauntered to the den, her hips swaying.

Batting minus zero, Medeci, the voice in his head mocked. No need to rub it in. He'd acted like a royal jerk, but the woman pushed his buttons royally. He tossed the blooms in the sink, filled it with water, and turned the tap off with such force it nearly came unhinged. Muttering an epithet, he yanked the fridge door open and icy air slapped him in the face.

Not since he'd been a boy had hunger pangs assaulted his body. He groaned, his stomach twisting and his mouth going dry. He was starving for this pale, honey-colored girl he'd married. He'd given her everything, including his name. He wanted to protect her, pamper her, love her … and she preferred to work for tips in that dive and live in that dump than with him. Where had he gone wrong that she had such an opinion of him? Air spun in his ribcage, his chest expanded, and he exhaled, defusing the pressure. He should send her packing and be done with this whole fiasco. But the promise of one more sexual encounter, at her request, plus the lesson he set in motion, were both much too tempting. This short time should zip by. He'd have her out of his heart long before then. *Sure thing, Doc.* Shut up!

He grabbed a sandwich, booted the refrigerator door closed with his heel, and stomped to his study.

* * *

Ellie marched to the bar, confiscated the bowl of pretzels and doing an about-face, marched to the couch. She plunked down, snatched a handful, and stared into the hearth. His words had knocked her off-center and if she hadn't grabbed the banister, she would've slithered to the floor in shock. The twisted snacks in her palm reflected her insides. She stuffed some in her mouth, the salty taste stinging the gash in her heart. But she crunched down, imagining that it was a part of his anatomy she'd bitten into.

By eclipsing her first singing gig, he'd blocked her source of income, meager as it was, making her solely dependent on him. Something she no longer wanted to be. And, he dared insinuate that he would do it again.

Proving that he disregarded her musical talent in lieu of his political ambitions. How high was the top for Peter? And what … who else would he trample on to get there? Seemed he was even willing to sacrifice their marriage to attain the pinnacle of success.

A sour taste filled her mouth and she forced the food down before she choked on it.

It had been a critical time to prove herself as an artist on the job, and he shouldered his way in—her thoughts shifted—what was he doing fraternizing in *The Blue Room*? With the pending election and his competitors stoking ammo against him, surely *The Blue Room* was not a place he wanted to be associated with. Bad press could derail not only his medical career, but his political aspirations.

He could've easily sent someone else to find her. Why had he come himself? Unless it was to ensure Louie didn't re-hire her.

Perplexed, she shook her head. She should just up and leave, this time for good. But proving she could resist him and make it on her own was far too tempting. She'd go right after she gave him a dose of his own medicine.

This interval should whip by soon enough. Her heart jammed in her ribs and she fisted her hand, pulverizing the pretzels in her palm. She dragged herself off the sofa and stepped behind the bar, dumping the snacks in the trash bin. Dusting crumbs from her fingers, she walked back and settled on the couch to watch TV.

After a couple of hours, Ellie flicked off the remote and, yawning, walked from the room. She trudged up the stairs and paused at the top to glance back down at the light shining beneath his office door.

She'd been here less than a day and Peter had already locked himself behind closed doors. If that's how he wanted it, fine by her. It'd save her the trouble of finding ways to avoid him. On the other hand, if this was a sample of things to be, she wouldn't get to show him how self-reliant she'd become without him. So much for her plans.

* * *

Peter leaned back in his chair, raised his arms, and stretched. Time he called it a day, and went to see what Ellie was up to. He clicked off the desk lamp and opened the door to a dark house. A sigh pitched from him. After his eyes adjusted to the shadows, he crossed the foyer and lumbered upstairs to his room … their bedroom.

Once inside, the walls seemed to close in around him and, groaning, he strode to the window. He shoved aside the sheer curtains she'd chosen and glared up at the moonless sky. It matched his mood. He heard her moving in the adjoining bedroom and went rigid. She was so close, but untouchable.

When he'd left the kitchen to walk to his study, he'd caught a glimpse of her lounging in the den like she'd already dismissed their earlier confrontation—dismissed him. A low growl built in his throat. Only a few hours had passed since she'd come home with him and she'd already barricaded herself behind closed doors. If that's how she wanted to play it, fine by him. At this rate, though, he wouldn't get close enough to hold her hand, let alone—he slammed the brakes on the erotic images. So much for his plan to love her and leave her.

Peter released the double-layer curtain and rolled his shoulders, easing tension. Two steps took him to the bed. He tore off his clothes and fell upon it, the squeak of the mattress spring perforating the silence. Soon as his head hit the pillow, he was out.

After what seemed only moments, Peter blinked, and then kept his eyes closed. It couldn't be morning already. His fatigued body rebelled at the thought. Then, he heard the sound that had awakened him.

Singing.

He must be dreaming. Of course he was. A melodious sound drifted up the stairs and into his room, wrapping around him like a warm hug. He cracked one eye open, then the other. All hell rushed into his mind. He groaned and hauled himself from bed; naked as the day he was born. He staggered into the bathroom and turned on the shower.

Within ten minutes, he slipped on a pair of jeans, a matching shirt, and, with socks and sneakers on his feet, bounded down the stairs.

He walked into the kitchen and came to an abrupt halt. "Goo-ood morning."

Ellie turned, defusing a lilting tune on her lips to a hum. A frilly apron was tied around her waist, her signature black leggings hugged her long shapely legs, and a pink pullover sweater dipped low at her cleavage.

Black ankle boots covered her feet, the black rim of her socks folded over the edge of the faux leather.

He stroked his chin. When did she start dressing so provocatively? Must've been her stint in that nightclub, he surmised, and set his mouth in a straight line.

"It is a great morning, isn't it?" She smiled and when she caught his surprised look, her smile widened.

After a sound sleep, Ellie had gauged her options and decided to make the most of each of the twenty remaining days in their agreement. She'd play the sweet wife to the hilt, bar intimacies. She'd show him what he was missing. When time was up, she'd leave, since he wanted it that way. *Thought you wanted it that way*, her mind mocked. I-I do. *Sure thing*. She dismissed the double-talk, but couldn't do the same with her fluttering pulse.

He looked fresh and sexy in his jeans, with his shirt stretching

45

taut across his chest. The damp curl falling over his brow tantalized and she took a step closer, but his next words halted her musings.

"It certainly is." He took a whiff of the brew percolating in the coffee pot on the kitchen counter. "Smells great."

She dropped rye bread in the toaster. "You want one or two eggs? Bacon?"

"Two." He straddled the chair at the small table in the corner of the room, normally reserved for the staff. "Bacon slightly crisped." He folded his arms across the back of the chair and focused on her curvy hips as she stood by the stove. "You don't have to do that."

A snooty lift of her chin. "I'm not helpless, Peter." She touched her bandaged temple with the spatula in her hand. "This is healing very nicely. It might even be better long before three weeks."

"You don't say?" He swept his eyes over her, settling on her cleavage, his meaning unmistaken.

She held the utensil up like a protective shield. "We agreed …"

His eyes darkened. "So we did." He drummed his fingers on the back of the chair. "Nothing said about looking."

"You're not looking. You're … you're …"

Amusement twitched the corner of his mouth, but he didn't help her out.

"You're ogling," she said, a warm blush tinting her cheeks.

"You didn't mind the sloshers at the club leering at you."

"I was too busy keeping track of my orders to be aware of anything else." She'd encased herself in a shell-shocked suit, served their drinks, and moved on to her next customer. The singing had been a lucky break when the regular chanteuse didn't show up—and an opportunity to make extra tips.

He lifted a brow. "But you're aware of me looking at you."

Yes, she wanted to sling back, her body thrumming at his nearness.

She'd always been aware of him, sensed him even when he wasn't in the same room. Aloud she said, "How could I not? You make it so obvious."

"You parading in that sexy get-up is what's obvious."

She opened her mouth, shut it, and then opened it again. "What're you insinuating?"

"Maybe you missed me?" He shuttered his gaze. "Missed ..." A provocative pause and—he pointed to himself and to her.

"You're delusional."

He laughed and the deep timbre of his voice vibrated around the kitchen. "You'll be asking me—"

She laughed and the sound tinkled in the air between them. "No."

"—before three weeks are up."

She tapped the spatula on the X on the calendar on the refrigerator. "Twenty days."

"Counting already?"

"If anyone's going to be on their knees, it's going to be you."

"I think not, *mia cara*." He reached for the carton of orange juice and bumped the rose array on the table. He poured a glass. "Want some?" he offered, his words loaded with innuendo.

"No, thanks." She scooped bacon onto a plate layered with paper towels to soak up excess oil. "I rescued them." She inclined her head toward the flowers on the table.

He chuckled and gulped down half the juice in his glass.

She cracked two eggs in the frying pan and the oil sizzled. "You want to eat in the dining room?"

She hoped not. She practically had to squint to see him sitting at the opposite end of the table, let alone have a conversation. The coziness of the kitchen was more conducive to a pleasant meal, but she rarely had access to it because it was denoted servants' turf.

"Naa." He nipped a piece of crisp bacon from the plate she carried to the table. "This is fine."

47

"Where are your manners?" She made to slap at his hand, but his reflexes were so fast, she missed.

"Gone out the window, when a man's hungry." He stuffed the strip in his mouth and rolled his eyes in appreciation.

She set a plate of eggs over-easy in front of him and a plate of scrambled at her spot. Scrambled. Exactly how her nerves were behaving, with Peter gazing at her with that glint in his eye.

Nights could prove more challenging. She buttered a piece of toast and wrinkled her brow. On the other hand, if Peter kept true to form, by the time he slogged home, he'd be so tired, he'd fall into bed. By then, she'd make sure she was good and tucked under the covers and sleeping in her own bed. That way, she'd only come across him for a couple of hours in the morning. A cinch. She could taste victory. A twinge pierced her chest, but she ignored it.

She spread strawberry jam on the toast and repeated the ritual with three more pieces. Then she started piling bacon on her plate. "Keep busy" was her mantra.

"You gonna eat all that?"

"No."

"May I have a piece?"

"You did already."

"I want another."

She passed him the plate; he took a piece and crunched it. "Mmm, good."

Ellie leaned across the table for the salt-and-pepper shakers and her breasts nearly spilled from the confines of her sweater. Bacon bits turned to mush in his mouth. He gulped. They'd fit so perfectly in his palms right about now. Soft and silky to his touch, taste of ambrosia in his mouth … he always wanted more … of her. He released a cramped breath. "Need any help?"

"No, thank you."

"You don't have to do this anymore." He picked up the coffee pitcher, went to fill her cup, but she declined. "I could recall the staff." He poured himself a cup of black brew, steaming flavor swirling upward.

"No." She smiled. "I can manage." She sprinkled a few grains of salt on the eggs on her plate. "I won't be here for that long."

Not only counting the days, but she was prepping for a hasty exit.

A hard line marked his jaw. He raised the cup to his lips and took a long swig of the bittersweet liquid.

"They deserve some time off." She poured ketchup over the food on her plate. "What … er … time will you be coming home tonight?"

"I'm here to stay."

The knife clattered on her plate, but she recovered it quickly. "What do you mean?"

"I'm long overdue for a vacation." He pierced a piece of egg with his fork. "Except for emergencies, I'm officially off duty."

She shot him a puzzled frown. "What about the election?"

"What about it?"

"Don't you have to be visible … at the hospital … make the rounds?"

"Nope." He set his gaze steady on her face. "I never let a formidable opponent know my next move." He clicked his tongue against his teeth. "Rattles 'em."

"Element of surprise and—"

"Yep."

"I see."

"I wonder if you do, Ellie." While he kept tabs on what went down in the medical community through his contacts, Peter did not intend to miss one day, one hour, one minute, one second with her. It could be the last they shared. He bit off a piece of toast, chewed, and wondered how he'd feel when he brought her to her knees. *It might be to your knees, buster,* the voice in his head challenged. Get lost.

Peter pulverized the food in his mouth. So many times he bent his knee for her—when he proposed, on their honeymoon, during the night alone in their bedroom trying to figure out what went wrong between them, and just the other day, cold and shivering, he'd slumped onto the couch, wondering if he'd ever find her.

She deserted him. And her stint in the club on the brink of this election could sabotage all he'd fought for these years. It could turn into a mud-slinging match unless he couped Louie's collection before he auctioned it to the highest bidder. Peter shoved the food down his throat. He had no intention of going on bended knee again. This time she had to come to him.

Chapter 5

After breakfast, Peter strode to his study, murmuring something about his medical journals. That hadn't surprised Ellie. What had knocked her for a loop was that he'd taken time off from the hospital for the three weeks.

Ellie strolled around the property, not sure what he was up to nor why, but certain it was more than it appeared. Scents of nature filled the air, mist fresh upon her face. A wobbly smile brushed her lips. Such a contrast from the traffic fumes and noise of her humble abode in North Hollywood.

During the time she'd been away, she'd lived from paycheck to paycheck, with no money left over even for a new lipstick. She had to admit she missed the comforts she'd known with Peter. But she was smart enough to know that resuming where they left off was not the solution to the woes of their marriage. She was a wife, not a bought woman.

She cringed. How could she not be 'a bought woman' in Peter's eyes, when he had paid for her parents' mortgage so they could keep their home, helped her father land a prestigious professorship, and lavished her with gowns, shoes, jewelry, and gifts galore. Is that why he treated her more like a mistress than a wife?

She bit her lip to stop its trembling. Had she been too naïve to realize that her innocent acquiescence, over time, would have ramifications that would spring a wedge between them? A sigh surged from inside her, and her shoulders slumped. A step, then another, and she paused, glancing about the luxuriant estate that was hers if she continued the role of the pampered woman. The trophy wife. Her heart balked. Never would she stoop to the level of gold digger, not even for her parents. And never would she sell herself to a man, even a man she adored, a man like Peter, whom she loved with every fiber of her being.

She squared her shoulders, tilted her chin in defiance and ambled on, the damp grass squelching beneath her boots. She brushed her fingers across the rose bushes, the scent a balm to her bruised spirit. A half-hearted giggle. Definitely, she'd have to set the man straight. And she knew how to do it.

But could she shake him from his complacency in three short weeks?

Compel him to see her as more than his sexual playmate? Or would he continue to be so absorbed in his profession, he'd remain impervious to her signals?

For certain, that would trigger the demise of their union.

She walked beneath a maple tree and a dewdrop fell smack on the tip of her nose, dispelling her troubling thoughts. Swiping the droplet with the tip of her finger, she licked it off, tasting freshness. She giggled and, twirling around, opened her arms wide, embracing all. For twenty more days, the fairy tale was hers for the taking and she'd play along. She set her mouth in a firm line. This time, she'd do it her way. As Ellie Ross Medeci and not simply as 'the model wife'.

A quick glance behind her at the big house, then, with a bounce in her step, Ellie followed the cobblestone path to the back yard.

* * *

Peter stood at the bay window of his study with an unopened file in his hand and watched her. She licked something from her lips and then, with a skip in her step, she rounded the corner out of sight.

Would Ellie ever understand his passion, his need to excel? In striving for the pinnacle, he could not be a regular stay-at-home guy, treading a nine-to-five cycle. That high level of success took sacrifice, brutal sacrifice. Ellie? Could he sacrifice his marriage to Ellie for the greater good? His gut recoiled. It would destroy him, but the alternative would be worse.

Don't be a noble fool. He shrugged the annoying words off.

He narrowed his eyes to laser-sharp slits. Maybe there was a way to have it all, including Ellie. A shadow flittered across his brain. But she'd have to want it as much as him and, for now, her actions signaled she was all for fleeing the 'castle' for good.

But he wouldn't give up without a fight—this, perhaps, could be the greatest battle of his life. Ellie or his noble mission?

His back muscles stiffened, his breath exploding from his lungs.

This interlude could very well prove a prelude to the end of their marriage. The thought stabbed his gut and he turned away, tossing the folder on the desk. He followed and plunked down in the swivel chair, rubbing the furrow between his brows with his thumb and forefinger.

He slapped the file open and drummed his fingers on the report, the furrow turning into a fully fledged scowl on his forehead. Would she ever look at him with that carefree gaze again?

The ringing of the telephone shattered his corrosive thoughts. "Medeci," he spoke into the speaker. A heavy pause, then he bit out, "How much?" He slammed his fist on the mahogany. "Highway robbery." He glanced out the window in the direction Ellie had disappeared behind the house. "Get 'em. And while you're at it, buy him out." A slow grin split his mouth. "Yeah, clean him out."

He slammed the receiver down and vaulted from his chair. *Dio mio*! He'd forgotten to tell Ellie about—

Her scream shot through him like a bullet.

He sprinted through the house and out to the grounds, skidding to a stop when he found her. Breath burned his lungs. She was pressed against the brick wall, trembling from head to toe, her face ashen.

"Down boy, down." Peter grabbed the Doberman Pincher by the collar and pulled him off her. The dog resisted and licked her hand, enjoying the taste of her. "King, down." With a firm tug, Peter controlled the animal. Ellie slid down the wall and landed on her tush on the grass before he could catch her.

"Ellie, I-I," Peter murmured, reaching out to touch her shoulder.

She flinched away from him and covered her face in her hands.

While the Doberman pranced around, vying for his attention, Peter kept his sights on Ellie. During an intimate moment early in their marriage, she confided to him that when she'd been eight years old, a thunderstorm spooked a neighbor's dog and he bit her leg. Since that time, thunderstorms and dogs immobilized her.

"Go-o away," she stammered.

He waited.

Slowly, she dropped her hands to her lap and shot him such a horrifying look of disbelief, he nearly stumbled back a step.

"Ellie, he's a puppy dog." Peter swallowed the constriction in his throat and patted the dog's head. The animal leaped up and licked his face.

"See?"

She shrank away and the dog did the same. Pushing against the wall, she stood and brushed at a stray curl on her brow. "Keep that brute away from me." She inched back toward the house.

"I'll see you in a few minutes." Peter watched her until she turned the corner. "Come on, King." He guided the animal to the doghouse he'd built.

One day, after Ellie had left—he toughened his jaw at the memory—he'd wandered the streets like a zombie. A loud yelping had pierced through the fog engulfing him, and he blinked at the pooch pawing the shop window. The pup looked at him with his big, doleful eyes and cracked the ice around his heart. Abandoned. Peter walked into the store and, moments later, walked out, clutching the warm bundle in his arms. The puppy licked his chin and he'd chuckled for the first time since Ellie'd left.

"Okay, boy, you're okay." Peter patted the animal's head and settled him in for the night, wishing he could say the same about himself.

The dog slurped his fingers and gave a woof, seeming to sense his dilemma.

"What am I going to do, mmm?" Peter ruffled him behind the ears.

The dog turned toward the house and barked several times.

"Go after her?"

King brushed against Peter's denim-clad leg and then dipped his head to the dish, crunching food pellets.

Peter smiled and headed for the house. Each step he took diminished the curve from his mouth until it became a hard line. Did she think him such a brute that he'd set King on her?

A faltering footstep gave him pause and he rubbed the back of his neck to ease a sore muscle. He breathed in the freshness of the late-afternoon breeze. Energized, he leaped up the veranda steps.

Once inside the house, he marched across the foyer and paused at the foot of the stairs. He glanced up in the direction of her bedroom. A muscle nicked his jaw. He took a deep breath, exhaled, and took the stairs two at a time. Striding down the hallway, he stopped in front of her door.

"Ellie."

Silence.

"Ellie." He knocked. "Are you in there?"

No answer.

Had she left? His stomach tensed, then relaxed. She couldn't have had time. He swept a hand through his hair and cleared his throat. "Let me explain." He rattled the doorknob and, at the same moment, she pulled the door open and he fell forward, grabbing for the doorjamb. Ellie raised her hands and blocked his headlong dive to the floor.

"No need." She yanked her hands away from his chest so fast an icy draft frosted the sizzle on her fingertips. "I intend to wash off the smell of dog." She wiped her hands on her bikini-clad hips. "And man."

"That's playing dirty, woman."

"Following your example." Her voice faltered. "You knew how I felt about dogs, and yet—yet—you—" She dashed past him, hiding her hurt.

"Ellie!"

She raced down the stairs.

"I didn't mean—" he bounded after her "—I forgot."

She paused at the bottom of the steps. "Forgot?"

"Yes," he confessed, reaching her side. "You don't think I'd stoop—"

"I don't know how low—"

"Enough." He took her arm and spun her around to face him. "You know better than that."

"Do I?

"In the confusion of your hospital stay, finding you, losing you—"

"That bothered you?" she whispered, watching him beneath her lashes.

He squeezed a little more on her flesh and then released her. The woman provoked him to hell and back. Maybe he should take her with him, give her a taste of the purgatory he'd gone through these last few months. Of course, he couldn't. A lesson, though, he could very well do, and rest easy with his conscience.

Wasn't that what this was all about, man? the voice in his head needled. *You bringing her here on a pretense of convalescing, thinking she'll come running back to you? Think, again.* She had him jumping hoops, but he determined to take control of the situation. *Precisely, the problem before.* Don't know what you're talking about.

He drew in a breath and expelled a whistle. "It was easy to forget—"

"Fine." She eyed him from head to toe and her nerves tingled with awareness. Warmth seeped into her. Her body craved his touch, his taste, his love. Of course, she couldn't give in to the temptation. If she did, she'd be playing right into his hands. "As I said, I need a wash." Abruptly, she turned and hurried through the open French doors to the swimming pool.

"Looks like rain."

She shrugged.

"I'll come with you."

"No." Then, she amended, "Please yourself." She didn't want him to think she couldn't handle being near him and wanting to … to … to … She shoved erotic thoughts far back in her mind and focused on the water.

"Don't get your bandage wet."

"I won't."

Cool air made her skin break out in goosebumps and she rubbed her hands over her arms. She dipped her toe in the shallow end. "Mmm, nice and warm."

"An illusion." He stepped behind her and his breath tickled her nape, making her insides toss with emotion.

"Must you stand so close?" She hopped aside and would've slid down the pool steps if he hadn't grabbed her around the waist.

"You have a problem with that?" He stroked her midriff across her navel with his thumb, sending her nerve endings into spasms.

"No," she said, too quickly. "I can be glued to you and not feel

57

a thing." *Not true*, her mind protested. Just to prove it, her heart-beat skipped and her stomach fluttered.

"Is that so?" He pulled her hard against him and his eyes drilled into hers, searching.

Time stood still.

"Ye-es." She caressed his cheek with her fingertips and steeling her nerves, pulled away from him. It cut her to the raw to do it, but it broke the spell. She couldn't let him see that he still rocked her emotions with one look, one word, one touch—one kiss. A whimper slipped from her mouth, and she waded into the water, praying he didn't hear.

She'd lived in his shadow for so long, she'd lost her personality and her individuality. In a sense, she'd lost herself in him. By the time she'd realized it, it had almost been too late. And so she left ... left him, to find herself. But he found her and brought her back ... to him, to his life ... for three more weeks.

If she yielded to him merely on a physical level this time, it would destroy her, and ultimately him. She'd feel guilty for not being strong enough to resist him and self-incriminate. He'd feel guilty for keeping her a prize possession and self-sabotage.

Ellie scooped water in her hands and let it glide over her arms. During this brief time, she had to show him that she was her own woman, and independent of him. Not simply an extension of him—a wife appendage to the doctor.

The outcome after three weeks would either be a real marriage or a quick divorce.

Chills shot through her, not from the weather, but from reaction to her turbulent thoughts.

It was a dangerous situation. She walked a fine line between determination and temptation. Another few moments, and she would've melted into his arms. His heart beating in time to her own, his mouth on hers, his tongue waltzing with hers, his hands touching, fondling her breasts, her ... she dipped down, and the water level reached her chin.

"How's the water?" Peter's voice sailed to her.

"Nice." She paddled further and floated on her back, the water cooling her flushed skin. Through her half-closed lids, she watched him.

He sat on the edge of a lounger with his legs slightly apart, his elbows on his knees and his hands steepled below his chin; his laser-sharp eyes on her.

Her gaze stumbled across the bulge between his legs, stretching the denim material taut across his thighs, and a jolt shot through her. Her pulse leaped and with it her temperature. She drew in a scalding breath and twisted away, swimming across the pool with a fluid front crawl.

Once Ellie reached the opposite end of the pool, she grabbed the edge and took a moment to regulate her breathing. Then, she pushed back from the side with her feet and frolicked in the water. In the background, the beast barked and her muscles tightened. Beyond that, the blare of a car horn sounded, and she relaxed. Not so isolated after all, although she often felt that way behind the wrought-iron fence.

"You've been in for fifteen minutes." Peter stood and stepped to the edge of the pool. "Come out, Ellie."

"In a minute."

Peter shuttered his eyes, watching her splash in the depths and his mind drifted to another time, another place …

"Come on, Doc." She'd giggled against his mouth and the tip of her tongue brushed his lips. "You can do better than that." With her arms wrapped around his neck, she peered at him through her gold-tinted lashes, half teasing and half inviting.

"That I can." He chuckled, but his heart was in his throat.

In that breathless moment, she let him go and scampered to the beach, her hair bouncing across her shoulders, her hips swaying in the night breeze.

She wanted to play, did she? Well, he was game.

While surf pounded the shore, he chased after her, his feet

59

sinking in the sand and sea spray cooling his skin. He snatched her up in his arms and her laughter rang in harmony with the ocean's concerto.

"Putting me to the test, woman?" He grinned, and holding her squirming body against his chest, waded out to thigh-deep water.

"Now Peter, I was only kid—"

Chuckling, he dunked her in the waves. She screeched and went under, a moment when his heart seemed to stop, and then she came up spluttering, fawn-brown eyes fuming. Before her verbal bullets peppered into him, he hauled her hard against his heart and tasted the heat of her lips.

Ellie moaned into his mouth. Deepening the kiss, he lifted her in his arms and walked from the waves, sea foam lapping at his ankles. He nibbled across her cheek and down her chin, nuzzling her nape, tang of sea salt teasing his taste buds.

"Oh, Peter?"

He licked, stroked and feasted on the pulse point of her throat. "Mmm."

"I seem to have lost my bikini top in the frolic with the waves."

He came up for air. "Saves me the trouble."

"It was my favorite—"

"I'll buy you another." He laid claim to the sensitive spot at the base of her neck, savoring the sweet taste of her with his tongue. "Two, ten, a hundred," he breathed against her damp skin, then traveled back to her mouth. "Whatever you want."

She'd whispered something against his lips, but it had gotten lost in the rush of emotion. He devoured her with his mouth, his tongue. A fevered moment, and she slid her tongue over his, teasing, stroking, loving him … he plunged deeper, a captive to the sensual feel of her. Blood pulsed through his veins, fueling his sex. He groaned with need. He wanted more, so much more …

A deprecating laugh sounded, and he realized it had come from him. Ellie still splashed at the opposite end of the pool, and his mind wandered back …

60

After a whirlwind visit with his family in Rome, Peter had whisked her off for a weekend honeymoon to the Italian Riviera. It had been brief because he had to return to work in the States, but it had been potent. A mere brush of her lips had him sizzling. When she snuggled against him, the lilt of her voice fanned the inferno inside him, making him feel like the sexiest man alive.

To the tune of waves lapping the beach behind him, Peter had trotted to a palm tree and laid Ellie on the large white towel spread beneath. Moonlight glinted on her moist body, casting a glow across her breasts and a tantalizing shadow between her thighs. She bent a knee and curled her scarlet-tipped toes in the sand, her sultry gaze, half innocent and half siren.

Intoxicating. His heart turned to mush and his sex rock-hard.

He gulped down the overwhelming emotion, but didn't fully make it. "*Bella*, Ellie," he murmured, falling to his knees beside her.

To regain control, he grabbed a towel from her beach bag and began blotting sea dew off her face. He worked his way down her body, his breathing picking up speed. "My Ellie."

When he reached her breasts, he knew he'd lost the battle. One mound filled his palm and, bending his head, he feasted on her nipple until it turned hard between his teeth. With fever rising, he slid his mouth to her other breast, swirling his tongue around the straining tip, until it too went rigid. Still hungry, he pulled it full into his mouth, suckling.

Ellie moaned with delight and held his head to the spot, her fingers sliding through his hair at the nape of his neck. "Peter, my love."

His hot breath fanned her breast, and he slid the towel down her cleavage to her abdomen. His mouth followed the path and settled on her navel. He dipped the tip of his tongue in the crevice, skimmed the terry cloth across the dark shadow below, and then tossed it over his shoulder. Inching his way lower with his mouth, he buried his face in her feminine curls. He nibbled closer, his hands gliding over her legs and nudging them apart. He fell into her and tasted her sweet musk flavor.

"Peter," she gasped, bucking beneath him.

"I'm here, *amore mia.*"

He tossed off his swim trunks and straddled her. Then, he stretched over her and branded her with his heat; his chest pressed against her breasts, his hips settled against hers, his steel length pushing against the apex of her thighs, his legs anchoring hers.

He trailed his fingers along the sensitive zone of her elbow to her wrist and shackled both her wrists in his grip. Her breasts rose and fell beneath him, and his heart battered his chest. Extending the moment to an explosive pitch, he raised her arms above her head and held her captive, his hot gaze probing deep into hers. He lowered his head and plundered her mouth, his tongue plunging deep inside, tasting, seducing, mating with hers.

X-rated sensation fueled him. He released her wrists and fondled her breasts, sliding his leg between her thighs. His hand glided lower, his fingers slipping inside her slick core, touching, stroking, stimulating.

Ellie arched into his hand and held him so tight her nails dug into his shoulders. But he welcomed the stimulant. Her scent, her feel, her taste ... wrapped around him until he could hardly breathe. Desperate to fill her with himself, he withdrew his hand and raising himself slightly, slid his steel length inside her. He nearly cried for the killing bliss of it, feeling like he'd finally come home.

Ellie sighed into his mouth and wrapped her legs around him, driving him deeper into her warm folds. At first, he took it slow, riding her to the serenade of the sea. When sea foam surged and collided with the rocks, he thrust into her, catching her sliver of pain in his mouth. She held him like she'd never let go, and he took courage, riding her to the crest. For a breathless moment, he felt suspended in eternity, like he'd die in her arms.

Waves crashed against a sand dune and she shuddered beneath him, then his own release came.

"Peter, my love," she whispered against his lips.

Still joined to her, he drew her closer into his embrace and, brushing a wayward curl off her brow, nestled her head against his thudding heart.

"I can feel your heartbeat," she whispered.

"I hope so." He smiled, the sweet taste of her still fresh upon his tongue. "You can't get rid of me so easily."

"Mmm, good thing that." Ellie twitched her nose at the fuzz on his chest tickling her mouth and tasted her way to his nipple. She nipped it with her teeth until it pebbled, then suckled it. The erotic sensation rocked him, and he groaned as an erection on another part of his anatomy made itself known. She dallied with his other nipple until it hardened between her fingers, then she slid her hand down his torso. She dipped a moist fingertip in his navel and when he sucked in a breath, she followed the spear of hair pointing lower, much lower.

She tangled her limbs with his, pulling him further inside her moistness. She lifted her lashes and her gaze locked with his. He glimpsed passion and vulnerability in her eyes and, at that moment, he knew he could not love her more. She was knitted to his soul.

"Ellie ..." he grunted, but couldn't voice all he was feeling. Emotion swelled inside him and rendered him speechless. A groan erupted from him and he cupped her buttocks, pressing her hard against his solid strength, friction birthing wave upon wave of exquisite sensation.

Surf smashed upon the shore and he thrust deeper inside her again and again ...

Ellie's laughter pulled him from his tumultuous reverie, and he heaved several breaths to control his racing pulse. "Time, Ellie."

"In a minute, Peter." She blinked her waterlogged lashes at him, fighting a memory knocking at her mind. It had been so long ago that first time with him, yet now, watching him stand guard over her, made it seem only like yesterday …

Ocean breeze had sailed through the secluded cove and ruffled palm fronds high above them. Half in shadow, Peter leaned into her and she'd reached up to him, the gold band on her finger glinting on a moonbeam. Such intense emotion filled her that she could hardly breathe. He whisked off his briefs, tossing them behind him, and she stared at him in awe. She sucked in a mouthful of air and her heart hammered in anticipation.

Tentatively, she reached out to touch him and when he gasped her name, she became bolder, taking him full into her hands. She stroked his length and he surged in her palm. Planting her lips against his heart, she kissed her way down his body, her tongue teasing his navel and licking a moist path lower to the prize in her hands. Air constricted in her throat and hot sensation spiraled inside her. She loved every inch of this man God had given her.

A whimper vibrated in her throat and Peter gripped her shoulders, lifting her face to his. He devoured her with his mouth and tongue, electrifying every nerve in her system and rocking her world. Then, he'd said something about buying her a hundred bikinis … and all she wanted was him. Only him …

Raindrops splashed her face and pitter-pattered on the surface of the pool, shattering her sensual fantasy. Ellie stuck her tongue out, catching nature's dew and signaled with her hand. "I'm coming."

Peter stood like an avenging angel at the shallow end, his gaze glued on her; at her words, tension seemed to have eased from his shoulders. Reluctantly, she swam toward him, each stroke bringing her closer to the inevitable clash between them.

Taciturn but ever vigilant, he paced her approach, tapping his foot on the tile to the rhythm of her crawl through the water. "Good girl."

Huh! Good girl indeed. Doctor beware. She was about to morph into—

She jerked off beat half-way to him, frantically treading water and her thoughts disintegrated.

He narrowed his focus, alert.

She massaged her leg beneath the surface and stared straight at her husband, fear gripping her chest.

"Ellie?"

"Ah …" She went under, her words drowning in the depths.

"Ellie!"

She shot back up, arms floundering and splashing everywhere. "Pet-er!" Water sucked her under.

Before his next breath, Peter tore his shoes and socks from his feet, yanked his jeans off, ripped the shirt from his back, and dived into the water. His heartbeat seemed to detonate in his chest. If he lost her now … *Dio mio*, this wasn't happening.

She fought to come up for air, but something restricted her attempts. Her hair splayed around her like a halo, her features surreal. A breath, and Peter grabbed her, hauling her above the water surface.

Ellie sucked in mouthfuls of air and fought him. "No! No!"

"Stop it, Ellie!" He treaded water like a madman. "I've got you."

In her panic, she climbed all over him and pushed him below the surface. He shot back up and gulped for air. A critical moment and, God forgive him, he backhanded her across the face. That snapped her out of it and dazed, she touched her cheek. A second later, her features crumbled and her tears blended with the chlorinated water on her cheeks.

"I'm sorry, *carina*," Peter held her tight against his chest and swam to the shallow end. "So, sorry." He lifted her in his arms and, stepping from the pool, laid her on the tiled floor. He knelt beside her and checked her vital signs. "You okay?"

She coughed. "I-I-I think so."

He snapped up the white towel from the lounger and wrapped it around her. "What happened?"

"M-my leg gave out."

"Cramp?"

She nodded. He stroked her calf with his fingers, his gentle, yet firm, touch working magic.

"Seems a little tight." He continued massaging the spot and heat from his fingertips penetrated her knotted muscle, easing the ache.

His ministrations affected other parts of her anatomy, and even in her distressed state, Ellie couldn't ignore her breathless reaction.

"Feel better?"

"Ye-es."

When she made to sit up, he scooped her up in his arms and strode into the house. He crossed the foyer and climbed the stairs, heedless of water streaming behind, staining the Persian carpet.

Peter marched along the upstairs hallway, hesitated for a second, and then opted for his bedroom.

"Please, no," Ellie murmured in protest.

"Go easy, Mrs. Medeci," he said, voice gruff. "No ulterior motive. Want to get you in top form before—"

"We get a divorce," she finished for him.

He tightened his mouth and made no reply.

His silence cut her so deeply that a groan tore from her. She turned, evading his probing gaze and hoped he thought it a result of her injury. Pain of a different sort settled around her heart and, swallowing back tears, she chastised herself for embarking on this dangerous interlude with him. He could break her heart all over again. She stiffened in his arms. Time she went on the offensive against this man, her husband.

Chapter 6

"Leg give you trouble before?"

"No."

"Sure?"

She nodded.

He placed her on the bed in a manner he'd use with any other patient. Impersonal. On their bed. Where they shared the most intimate moments between husband and wife. She squirmed at the memory, her heart aching.

She shut her eyes. He was so close; she'd seen the deep blue of his irises, the length of his lashes. She could reach out and touch him, smooth the crease above his brow, caress his cheek, rough with five o'clock shadow, outline his lips that had created such magic on her own. An agitated sound worked its way in her throat and she squashed it by squeezing the bedspread in her fists. The sensual feel of satin beneath her fingers was a tempting reminder of how she loved him. Anytime, anyplace and however he wanted it. Her body connected to his, her heart attuned to his, her soul aflame with his.

Shivers shook her. Mere inches from her, he might as well have been ten thousand miles away. She had better accept that these weeks were the last she'd share with her husband. She hardened her resolve; she'd not come out a casualty of a marriage 'war'. With that thought to sustain her, Ellie opened her eyes and collided with his dark gaze.

"Ellie," Peter whispered, his breath fanning her brow. A muscle ticked at his jaw and she reached up to smooth it, and then, checking the motion, let her hand drop by her side. She blinked, thinking she must've mistaken the raw hunger in his gaze. Her shocked nervous system must be playing tricks on her jittery emotions. She parted her lips to release pent-up air in her lungs, and he descended.

A warning clanged in her brain.

She should push him away, but it had been so long. He bent his head and a droplet from his still wet hair landed on her cheek and slid down to nestle on the corner of her mouth. She flicked her tongue out and licked it away. A guttural sound erupted from him, his mouth now a bare whisper from her own … his naked body, bar his briefs, that left nothing hidden, still moist from his dunk to fish her from the pool. She closed her eyes, anticipating the feel of his mouth on hers, his tongue sliding over hers, tasting—

You'll be begging me. A tremor zipped through her and her eyes shot open wide. She placed her hand flat on the center of his chest. "Go away."

Stunned for a heartbeat, he still held onto her, his words icing her flesh. "Sure thing, *principessa.*" He drew in a sharp breath, his face a mask of contradicting emotions—bewilderment, hurt, desire, confusion, and anger. But he let her go so fast she slumped back against the pillows, the imprint of his hands branding her bare shoulders. He hauled himself off her, cast a last cursory glance over her and stalked to the adjoining bathroom. "I have some salve to ease the pain of your leg."

But would do nothing for her heart. "You struck me."

"What the—" He paused in stride, turned to face her, and his gut kicked. The flimsy bikini she wore defined her every curve, the swell of her breasts, her nipples straining against the wet cloth. His narrowed focus drifted to her midriff, tripped over her navel and zoned in at the triangular shadow between her thighs.

A growl built in his throat. He made to turn away, but his gaze ricocheted to the curve of her leg, over the high arch of her foot to her scarlet-tipped toes. The rough sound inside him built momentum ... sexual reaction had every muscle in his body tense, he was hard as iron ... a step or two and he could be sliding inside her, her slick softness like heaven ... moving ... plunging into her ... fondling her ... smothering her pleasured moans with his mouth ... about to explode inside her—

The growl blasted from him in a grunt, defusing the sexual pressure inside him and hurling him headlong into harsh reality. He dreamed of a forever with her and had tried his damnest to give her everything. But she'd tossed it back in his face. It hadn't been enough for her.

Could he have been so wrong about her? Had she hooked him to bankroll her parents out of poverty? Was she playing coy, with her running away, to see how much more she could get out of him? And yet, she'd never asked him for anything; he'd helped her family of his own free will. Could that have been her subterfuge?

Doubts plagued his mind. Totally unacceptable to him, a man of hardened confidence, a man in charge. Definitely, he'd have to get the lady to confess, and soon. A sly curl to his lip. And he had the means to do it.

He brushed his fist across his mouth, smothering a near snort of a laugh. It had been a mirage ... an illusion that shattered, but he still wanted her. He was a fool. If he didn't take control of his passion, it would destroy him and all he worked, no, slaved, to build ... for her ... for them. Sweat dampened his chest and he clamped his teeth against the rip in his gut. After five years, it was coming to an end. A cold death-like end. Time he accepted it, but not before he had one more time with her.

"I slapped you" – his eyes drilled into hers – "because you would've drowned us both."

"You had no right—"

"I had every right if it meant saving your life … and mine."

She closed her eyes and a tear oozed between her lashes. He took a step closer, wanting to kiss it off her cheek … brush the curls plastered across the bandage at her temple. An abrupt halt. Would he ever learn? If he touched her now, it'd be the end of him, and that's not how he planned it.

She'd ask, he'd take, and then discard. His jaw turned granite. She had to ask him. And he'd make sure she did.

He gulped down bitter taste, blistering his throat and souring his belly. He was behaving like a stranger to himself and to her and that was the biggest illusion of all, for the more he resisted, the more his body craved, his sex hard and ready for her. He inhaled a rush of oxygen. He'd wait it out. Have her where he wanted … under him, on her knees, begging him—

Abruptly, he strode into the bathroom, his usually generous heart turning cold with his savage thoughts. He shoved his emotions aside, put them under lock and tossed away the key. The impersonal Doc was who he'd become. An act he perfected over the years when dealing with the most difficult patients and the medical politicians who poked around for any dirt to oust him. On their top ten most-wanted list for no other reason than him bucking the system, Peter, in making a surprise bid for the Chair, was betting to beat them at their own game.

Yes, definitely, he could carry out the ruse with his … er … wife.

Peter marched across the room back to her side. "Here." He tossed the jar of salve into her hands. "Smooth some of this on your leg. It'll soothe the strained ligaments." Noting dampness on her cheeks, he set his mouth in a hard line. "Tears are a reaction from shock."

Ellie nodded, accepting his prognosis and twisted the lid. The stubborn thing wouldn't open.

"Oh, give it here." Peter grabbed it from her and wrenched it open. A pause, then he dipped his fingers in the gook and smoothed it on the back of her leg. High voltage charged into him, his intake of breath a sharp sound. He exhaled between his teeth and ignoring the fever escalating between them, massaged the ointment on her skin.

Ellie closed her eyes for a heart-stopping moment. Then, she lifted her lashes and placed her hand over his. "I can do it, thanks."

He shrugged and, stepping back, slumped onto the chair by the dresser, allowing residue salve on his fingers to air-dry. Through his half-slitted eyes he watched her take over where he left off, the circular motion of her fingers upon her flesh, mesmerizing. He swallowed the acrid taste in his mouth. Seemed she couldn't stand to have him touch her, even in a professional way. He smirked. Who was he kidding? Her heat infused him with cataclysmic awareness. Touching her could never be anything but personal … intimate … potent. He shook his head. *Snap out of it, Doc.*

"Have you ever had an injury to that leg?"

"No." Her hand stilled over the muscle. "Yes. I mean it was so long ago, I almost forgot."

"What?"

"This is the leg th-the dog bit."

"That could explain it," he said.

"What?"

"Thinking King attacked you brought it all back in your psyche."

"I don't understand," she said.

"The cramp could've been psychosomatic."

"Psycho—what? She smoothed more lotion over her leg.

"A past trauma aggravating your emotions when you're confronted with a similar situation."

"I'm a grown up girl, *dottore*," she chuckled. "Please save your

71

psychoanalysis for your other patients."

He steepled his fingers and rested his chin upon them, his gaze shadowed. "And are you?"

"What?"

"A grown-up girl."

"Ye—" She stilled her fingers over the slippery gook on her leg and glanced up, colliding with the intensity of his eyes. "What are you getting at, Peter?"

He eased himself from the chair, his hot gaze gliding over her, his meaning unmistakable. "When you're ready to play grown-up games, you be sure to let me know, mmm?"

"Get out!" He goaded her to boiling point and had her writhing in mortification—she'd been within a hair of taking him up on his offer.

A disaster that, indeed. She couldn't fall into the temptation and walk away from him as she planned. Fury overrode the sexual catalyst and she imagined all sorts of scenarios where she cracked the whip and he came crawling to her … Stop! None of it was true, except the part where she wanted to clobber him and love him at the same time.

But, she had a plan to teach him a lesson didn't she?

"Sure thing, wife." He sauntered to the door.

"Don't call me that."

Her blatant denial lacerated his insides and he paused in stride for a millisecond. But you are that, *Signora* Medeci. And you will play the part to the very meaning of the word. He stalked out.

Chapter 7

Peter shoved his arms through a t-shirt and plodded down the stairs, a harsh sound ejecting from his chest at the irony of it all.

At nine years of age, he'd begun clawing his way up from the streets of Little Italy in New York. He managed his newspaper route in the early hours of dawn before going to class. After school, he delivered groceries, and in the evening bussed tables. It had been grueling for a young boy and although he'd been tempted with making a fast buck, he turned it down. Must have been his Christian upbringing—something about honest work and his word being good. After helping with household expenses, he saved any remaining pennies for his future studies in medicine. That, and an academic scholarship, had given him the chance to escape a hand-to-mouth existence.

His profession and his strategic global investments had paid off. A self-made millionaire, he'd become a haven for some and a target for others. He curled his lip in distaste. Which one was he to Ellie now? The answer eluded him.

In three long strides he reached the closet in the foyer and grabbed his leather jacket off the hook. Shoving his arms through the sleeves, he marched to the front door and yanked it open.

He stepped outside and slammed it shut, the sound reverberating with finality behind him.

Peter stood on the veranda and breathed deeply the fresh, damp air of twilight. Scent of roses reminded him of her ... her perfume. Wound up like a spring ready to snap he leaped the three steps to the concrete walkway. Air hurled from his lungs. He stuffed his hands in his pockets and glanced up at clouds matching his mood. Hunching his shoulders against the nip in the air, he stomped to the back of the house and to his only friend.

"Hey, King." Peter got down on his haunches. "Come 'ere, boy."

The Doberman barked his greeting.

"You're about the only one who loves me, big pup." Peter ruffled his ears and the animal pawed his chest, slurping at his face.

Peter chuckled and the dog dropped his paws to the grass, looking up at him with soulful eyes. "Thanks," Peter murmured, wondering if the canine's woebegone expression was a reflection of his own. "What's it all been for, mmm?" He grabbed the leash from inside the doghouse and, stroking the animal's neck, he hooked the leather strap on his collar. "The blood, sweat, and guts?"

While he'd slaved away to reach the summit of his medical career, Ellie lazed her days away like a pampered princess ... his *principessa*. He guffawed. Except, she ditched him and fled the 'castle'. His facial muscles tightened—seemed she no longer wanted him. A growl shot from him and King barked. "It's okay, boy," he said, patting the dog's head. Except, of course, it wasn't.

Turning up his collar against a sudden gust of wind, Peter walked the dog around the grounds and carried on a one-sided conversation. "Didn't it matter to her that I worked so hard?" The dog gave him a sympathetic woof. "Didn't she care?"

If he stopped working at this break-neck speed, he feared he might backslide into failure. Need. Hunger. And he could never allow that. Scars of poverty had embedded themselves in his psyche and he was driven to succeed at any cost. *Including the cost of your marriage to Ellie?* The thought whipped through his mind, but he shut it up. Too many people depended on him. His patients, his family, and he thought Ellie. But, it seemed she didn't want what he had to offer.

"What am I missing here, King?" He stroked the dog's glossy coat with his hand and the animal brushed against his jean-clad leg. If he gave in to her demands to become a more regular stay-at-home guy, he'd never be able to retain his position at the top.

Resentment would rear its ugly head, gnawing at his gut. He'd be torn between his wife and the need to excel beyond the norm. And what would it do to her? Turn her into a bitter shrew?

Peter shoved a hand through his wind-tossed hair and sighed. He was at a crossroads. In less than three weeks, he had to make a life-altering decision. His pulse jogged. He might be forced to choose between his profession and his wife ... something he couldn't fathom at this moment.

King jerked the leash and, sniffing the grass at the base of an oak tree, distracted Peter from his musings.

"Come on, boy." Peter unhooked the strap from the animal's collar. "I'll race you to the fence."

After a couple of laps, Peter settled the animal in for the night and trudged back to the house to the encouraging sound of barking.

Heck, if he was going to end up in the doghouse himself, at least he had company. Grinning, he climbed the steps and crossed the veranda to the front door. He turned the handle. He frowned. He twisted, jiggled, and yanked at the brass knob.

"No." He shook his head. "Impossible."

A wistful twist marred his mouth. The way he'd bolted from

the house should make this no surprise. Of course, he could pound on the door, signaling Ellie to come downstairs and let him in. He hesitated. Would she? Or would she ignore him? His pride had taken enough hits these last few weeks, not to mention the pummeling today. On the other hand, if she was asleep, he didn't want to wake her.

Kicking the door down was a possibility. He pursed his lips and, deciding against it, leaned back against the wall. A deep sigh, and he slid down, landing on his backside and propping his elbows on his bended knees. Spending a cold night on the veranda wasn't an option. He cleared his throat and leaped up, walking the circuit twice, searching for a way to break in.

He locked his fingers, stretched, and his knuckles crackled. He'd have to climb the oak tree to his bedroom and hope no one mistook him for a burglar. That's all he needed to add to his woes; his mug shot splattered all over the newspapers, stashing the vultures' arsenal who were 'gunning' for him.

"No way," he muttered.

He stood at the foot of the tree and glanced upward. As a kid, he scrambled up bigger ones and although he'd gotten bumped and bruised, he found the climb to the top exhilarating. He calculated the odds at his age, now thirty-three. With no other alternative, he shrugged from his jacket, tied it around his waist, and jumped, clutching the lower limb.

"Gotcha!" He hauled himself up and straddled the sturdy branch. It held his weight and he breathed easier. Swiping foliage out of his way, he continued climbing.

When he neared the top, the clouds burst in a sudden shower and soaked him. "What's happened to the California sunshine?" he grumbled, thinking even the weather was against him.

He blinked raindrops from his lashes and reached for the window ledge. A twig gouged a hole in his shirt; he missed the mark and ended up with a handful of leaves. A growl shot from deep in his throat and he shimmied closer along the branch. He grabbed the next one up, and balancing like a high-wire act, stretched out, seizing the window molding.

Unlocked. Relief coursed through him and he slid the pane open, glad he decided against window screens. He pulled himself onto the ledge, wiggled through the gap, and landed with a thud, curtains wrapping around him. Impatiently, he shoved them aside and squinted in the shadowed room.

He heard the rhythm of Ellie's breathing. Good, she was asleep. He didn't want her witnessing his humiliation, yet again. But wanting to check on her, he stepped closer and an x-rated expletive burst from him. Air blocked in his chest and his heart thudded. He snapped into action.

* * *

Several hours later, Ellie fluttered her lashes open. She moved her leg, felt no pain, but felt him. Realizing she was nude, she groaned and turned over, her gaze clashing with her husband's amused eyes.

"What are you doing here?" she asked, tone accusing.

"Sleeping."

"Bu-ut, you're not supposed to—"

"With you?" He bent his elbow and supported his chin in his hand. The motion only made the sheet ride low on his waist, tantalizing her with what lay hidden beneath.

"Ye-es." So sexy, this man she married. Dark hair swirled at the center of his chest, then streaked down his navel and beyond to what was hidden beneath the bed sheet. She swallowed. He'd filled her hands and she teased him with her fingers, playing, touching, stroking—the memory shot a dart into the center of her heart ... she ached ... for him. He lay so close, hair on his thigh grazed her leg, but distance wedged them apart. "We agreed."

"So we did."

"You didn't keep your word."

77

"That I did, *mia cara.*" He lowered his lashes a fraction. The sheet slipped lower with every agitated word she spoke, and he zoned in on the swell of her breasts. He ran his forefinger over her shoulder and reached up, smoothing a curl behind her ear. "I didn't touch you."

She drew away. "I don't have any clothes underneath this sheet."

He laughed. "Not a first, surely, Ellie?"

"That was different—"

His eyes darkened. "How so?"

"We were … I mean you and I … we were—" A hot wave tinted her cheeks and she blinked her confusion.

"Making love."

Erotic images fleeted through her head and to shut them up, she said, "You had no right to undress me, Peter." She hadn't imagined him.

During her restless sleep, she felt his warm hands defuse iciness from her body. She'd curved closer to his heat, and when he lifted her head to remove her top, she opened her eyes for a split second, but it had all been so fuzzy. Drowsy, she'd drifted off to sleep.

"I did it for your own good."

"Oh?" She brushed a hand across the dry bandage at her temple.

"When I stumbled into the room—"

She arched a golden eyebrow.

"Never mind." He shook his head. "You were shaking, your teeth chattering. Running a fever."

Silence.

"I figured you'd change before falling asleep."

"I intended to—"

"I had to get you out of that damp bikini. Get you under the covers. Change the wet bandage. Keep you warm."

"Thank you," she murmured, her next words acerbic. "Did the remedy include you under the covers with me?"

"It did." He leaned closer, his scent titillating and his breath tickling her ear.

Dangerous.

"Hmm." Sensations she'd pushed far back in her psyche flared to life, but she resisted. She shoved him, but he stayed his claim.

"Woman, you were in shock." He spread his arms on either side of her and trapped her against his heart. Her breasts pressed against his chest.

Delicious.

"The fastest way to warm you was body heat to body heat."

"Is that what you're doing now?"

"Only if you want me to." His eyes hot with desire challenged her.

She writhed beneath him, wanting him to explore every curve, touch every inch, lavish every spot of her body with his mouth, his tongue; take her on a ride to the moon. Her mind balked and her heart throbbed. "Yes ..."

"Yes?" He held his breath, hesitated a second and exhaled a blast of air. Caressing wisps of hair off her brow, he placed his lips to the spot, his tongue teasing her skin. His mouth explored her temple, the curve of her cheek, the shadow of her throat. He cupped her breast.

Ellie closed her eyes. Just for a moment. His touch electrified every nerve in her body, creating a typhoon of emotion inside her. Her breath caught in her throat, her pulse raced, her stomach fluttered and her senses heightened. Sexual fantasy flared across her mind. He slid his leg between hers, his hair grazing her skin, his moist body heat gliding over her. Her limbs melted. Sensation shot through her. She wanted to—wanted him. How she wanted to let this moment take its course.

If she gave in now, she'd forfeit any headway she made in compelling him to see her in a different light. See her as more than his bedroom playmate. His property. Her mind besieged her heart. She might win this slam-bam-thank-you-ma'am night of passion with her husband, but ultimately she'd lose. Shallow puffs of air slipped between her lips. She'd lose herself to him. Lose him to his profession. Lose the marriage to sexual encounters with him.

In order to change the course of their relationship, she'd have to say no, even if every fiber of her being screamed yes!

Still hesitating, she licked her lips. He groaned. She gulped. Perhaps this once, she could give in. Oh, how she wanted, craved, his love, his sex.

She closed her eyes and remembered the gauntlet he'd thrown down. *You'll be asking for it, begging me.* Dear God, what had happened to them, their dreams, their life?

She stroked his cheek with her fingers, hating what she was about to say. "Yes ..."

He sighed into her neck, licked, kissed.

"... if that's what I wanted."

He froze. A rasping sound ripped from him and he flipped on his back. "But it's not ... what you want." His words forced, icy.

She didn't answer. Couldn't answer. Either way, she'd give herself away. She dared not even glance at him, for he'd see the mist glazing her pupils. "I-I have to get up," she murmured, her voice cracking.

"Your words say one thing, but your body another, dear wife." And to score his point, he reached over and brushed her nipple with his thumb.

That little bud shot to erection. Ellie groaned at her body's betrayal and, pulling the sheet over herself, turned away from him. She blinked, tears welling in her eyes. "Get out of my bed, Peter."

He chuckled, a dry sound. "Sure thing, *signora*." He slid from beneath the covers and walked to the window, dawn light glinting off his bronzed body.

Ellie curled underneath the satin sheets and watched him. He pulled the curtain aside and pondered the outdoors. She wondered what was going through his mind and if she had a place in his thoughts. He stretched his arms over his head that moments ago … a lifetime gone … had possessed her, and locked his hands behind his neck. The promise of magic his fingers could work over her flesh lingered in the air.

Ellie strobed her sights over his tight tush and down his muscular legs, which a heartbeat ago had anchored her beneath him. A stirring inside her. She made to glance away, but instead remained mesmerized by the bulge at the apex of his thighs. Although shadow camouflaged him, she knew his solid strength and sexual desire zapped inside her.

A loaded moment and he let the curtain fall back in place, the rustling sound like a caress, a lover's touch. He turned. She saw him full frontal and gasped. Her pulse scrambled, her body hot and moist. How she wanted … craved … he was hers for the asking … all she had to do … she moved beneath the covers … stopped. The price was too high … herself. *But then, what will your life be without him, mmm?* She pulled the covers over her head and eclipsed the warning.

A frustrated sigh escaped from deep within her and she flipped over, her fist pressed against her mouth, a whimper feathering from her lips.

"Som'm the matter?" He snatched his jeans from the corner chair, where he tossed them the night before.

"Go to he—"

"Been there," he murmured. "Wanna come along?"

"Oooh!" She pummeled the bed with her fists and heels.

"I take it that's a no." He grabbed his shirt and ambled toward the bathroom, whistling.

She gritted her teeth and tossed the sheet off her head. Whistling. Grr! At a time when every cell in her body seemed about to burst, he was behaving like he hadn't a care in the world. The man was driving her mad.

81

Whatever possessed her to stay with him for three weeks? *An excuse to teach him a lesson is why you agreed*, the voice in her head prodded. *Show him that you didn't need him*. Which was a joke. It was only the second day and her body throbbed with her need of him, his love. But was the feeling mutual? Or had she simply become a necessary addition for his career? After all, the 'right wife' could be an asset to an ambitious man like Peter. Of course, she'd been groomed to fit that role and gone along with the transformation for him. She stared at the sparkles on the ceiling, wondering why he'd chosen a plain girl like her …

It had been a stormy November night and she'd just entered the last book return in the library computer.

"Hello, Miss." She heard his voice, deep and mellow, drift to her and furrowed her forehead, busy stacking books on the trolley. "Sorry, we're closed," she said, without looking his way.

"This'll take just a sec." He rapped his fingers on the counter. "Do you have the medical journal by …"

She tapped her toe in impatience, glanced up, and got sucked into his midnight-blue gaze.

"… Kagen and Kagen?"

"Wha-at?" She swallowed the rest of her words and swiped her moist hands on her thighs. Her pulse rocked.

"Do you have—"

"Oh, I think so." She smiled at him. Hey, it wasn't everyday a sexy pinup boy strolled onto her turf. And a continental type to boot. She'd bet her meager paycheck that with his Italian good looks and hypnotic eyes he had more than one female head turning his way. But it seemed he was focused only on his errand.

"Where is it?" he asked, oblivious of the direction of her thoughts.

"Yes, of course … the journal." Her fantasies shattered, tinkling around her feet like a glass slipper. In looks, wealth, and station, this guy, with his designer shirt and gold watch strapped to his wrist, was light years from her sphere. And he looked only about twenty-eight.

At twenty-three, she shopped at the local Goodwill store and had to stretch her minimum wage salary to last the month. What she earned helped keep a roof over her and her parents' heads and paid for her baby brother's meds. Due to the economic downturn in the country, she was the only one bringing home any cash, and with the house in jeopardy, she had to cut costs where she could; that had included her studies in fashion design and marketing. But she'd never given up on her singing dream, for amidst the chaos of her life, it was the only thing that kept her sane. It cost her nothing, and she could belt out a tune in the shower, or while moonlighting at the local pub on weekends.

A wistful sound grazed her tongue.

He cleared his throat and she blinked. Unbelievable, but just for a second, she'd forgotten about this hunk in front of her. Now he commanded her attention once more.

"Oh, yes, the book." She grinned at pinup boy *numero uno*, and her hands trembled. Yep, no princess she, but here was Prince Charming in the flesh.

A sigh filtered from her mouth and he squinted at her.

Snap out of it, Ellie.

"Two aisles down on your left, near the back workstation." She pointed the way and pressed the stack of books to her bosom. Daydreams were a distraction and she nipped them from the get-go. She couldn't afford to get sidetracked by him, no matter his perfect ten packaging. She had to concentrate on her work … the job that paid the bills.

"I don't have time to scout for it." He batted the black lock flopping over his brow with an impatient hand.

"What are you doing here, then?"

A flitter of annoyance crossed his features, then he flashed her his killer smile, his dimple making her heart skip. "Would you find it for me?"

Okay, she'd play along. "What's it worth to you?" She fluttered her eyelashes at him.

You're going to get singed, girl.

She ignored the warning bombarding her brain. The bills were paid for the month, so she'd toss her angst aside; she'd enjoy this rich playboy's company for a few minutes to break the monotony of her life. Chances were she'd never bump into him again, so no danger.

No? The voice needled. She bashed it far and away into the dome ceiling.

"Hmm." He stroked his cheek, giving her the once-over. He spotlighted her eyes, her mouth … a pause at her bosom and then his blade-thin focus shot back up clashing with her raised eyebrows.

Heat spread over her body. She was thankful her body was hidden beneath a beige turtleneck sweater and matching mid-length skirt skimming the tops of her black boots. His silent scrutiny made her fidget, and she felt her face flaming. She twisted away from him and set the books on the trolley, her hair shielding her flushed cheeks.

Where had she gotten the nerve to flirt with him in this brazen way? The long hours on her feet, bored out of her wits, must've been the catalyst.

"I-I was only kidding." She turned back his way, hoping the blush staining her face had diminished. "If you wait a sec, I'll help you."

"No waiting," he demanded. "I have to get back to class for an exam." He heaved a sigh, but there was a twinkle in his eye. "Pizza and a movie this weekend."

"But I don't like pizza." Oh, she was bad. She loved pizza.

But he wasn't having any of it. "Get the book."

Okay, the fun had gone far enough. He had the look of a love 'em and leave 'em type. She'd not be his next target. "No thank you to your offer."

"I don't like to owe anybody." He rubbed his hand across the faint stubble on his jaw.

"You don't owe—"

"Find the book."

At her elevated brows, he added, "Please."

She nodded. "Yes, of course, sir."

His commanding tone had her prickling, but she found the book. He'd come back the next day for another journal ... the pizza and movie date advanced to dinner and dancing ... kissing and romancing ... and she'd married him ...

And from the get-go, he'd pursued his career with a vengeance. Now here they were, five years later, on the brink of divorce. Her heart sank.

Ellie shifted beneath the covers. She'd gone from a bored doctor's wife, to a *busy* bored doctor's wife, fluttering from luncheons to shopping sprees to medical events. She'd begun questioning herself, him, their relationship. She imagined a marriage where they'd share their lives, their dreams, and their future. Share an intimacy that was more than sexual.

Her temples pounded. How was this possible when he implied her career choice might cost him his? If that were to happen now, she'd hate herself. On the other hand, his unrelenting ambition might snuff out the hope of pursuing hers. If that were to happen, she'd not only despise herself but Peter too.

Ellie groaned from the depths of her being. They were on a collision course, and she feared there was no way to slam on the brakes. At a loss, she drew the covers up to her chin and held on tightly.

Just then, Peter walked in from the bathroom dressed in hip-hugging denims and a matching shirt, his hair damp. His feet were bare. Each step he took brought him closer. A lump of emotion had her nearly gagging, and she gulped it down. Her pulse sprinted.

"Hungry?" He paused at the foot of the bed, his eyes shadowed.

His aftershave wafted to her and wrapped around her frazzled nerves like a warm caress. So many times they shared the shower, laughing and loving beneath the spray. She set her mouth in a firm line, squashing the taunting memory.

"Marta left some frozen—"

"Go away."

Chapter 8

Peter chuckled, but it was a dry sound. "As you wish, *principessa*."

After he shut the door behind him, an oppressive silence smacked her. A moan ripped from her. Why had he called her princess? He used that in their most intimate moments.

Ellie shuddered. This cat-and-mouse game was tearing her apart. Denying yet wanting, craving him. She was like a junkie needing a fix—him. She had to get over it. *Wha-at? You want to get rid of something—this feeling everyone spends their whole life searching for? You've gone bananas, girlie*, the voice in her head muttered without apology.

She nearly snorted. It wasn't all sunshine and roses, not when one tall dark and very sexy Italian wanted to be in control ... of her life, their marriage, and unknowingly stifling her, except in the bedroom.

Even on the day she left, she tried to resist him ...

"Wake up, *principessa*." He'd stretched out on the king-size bed beside her and blown in her ear, his fingers flirting with the string of beads draped on her back.

She raised her hand from beneath the sheets and playfully swatted him. "Go 'way." She turned over, cuddling in the covers. "I want to sleep."

Chuckling, he flicked the satin sheets off her, hauled her into his arms, and she melted into his heat. He captured her mouth with his, his tongue slipping inside; gliding over hers in an erotic waltz … exquisite sensations buzzing through her. Her moan of pleasure tickled his mouth, and he blazed a trail downward, flicking his tongue over one nipple then nibbling his way to the other, before taking it full into his mouth.

She arched into him; with every cell in her body aroused, she wrapped her arms around his neck, her fingers weaving through his hair. "Peter." His name was a whisper from her lips.

Holding her so tenderly yet possessively, he'd branded her forever with his touch, his kisses, and his body. He lifted his head from the curve of her neck and captured her lips with his, his words a soft caress. "I love you, Ellie."

"Peter, my love." She breathed against his mouth, her hands stroking the muscles of his back.

"*Mia bella*, Ellie." He groaned from deep in his throat. "I don't ever want to lose you. You're mine."

"I am." She wrapped her arms tightly around him, holding onto him like a lifeline, and thinking she'd die without him.

She heard relief explode from somewhere deep inside him, and then he crushed her mouth beneath his to conceal his vulnerable moment. He blazed a path of fierce passion down to her navel, circled with his tongue, dipped into the crevice, and she pressed into him.

Delight shimmered through her, and he trailed his fingers lower, fondling her … she bucked into his hand … he stroked her more. Raising his head, he caught her cry of pleasure with his mouth, and then he slipped his hard length inside her, penetrating deep and high.

Taken over by him, Ellie molded her hands over his shoulders, her nails digging into his flesh, her legs wrapped around him, pulling him further inside her. She held onto him, fusing with him … one with him. He drove into her, and she hung on for the ride. His rhythmic movements inside her created exquisite friction and rocked her to the peak. Acute sensations spiraled, locked … she felt suspended on the brink, and then she went over the edge, shattering in wave after wave of bliss. A frenzied moment and he shuddered against her with his release, and together they floated from heaven to earth …

A tear slid beneath her lashes now, then another, and another, soaking the pillow she was hugging. She released a trembling breath. Staying in bed wouldn't make her problems go away. She'd have to get up and deal with her feelings, her marriage, her future with him or … her heart kicked in protest … without him.

So, what's your plan of attack? the voice in her head taunted. "Shut you up, for starters," she snapped and realizing she'd spoken out loud, cringed. Maybe she was losing it.

She pushed hair off her face, slid out of bed, and padded to the shower. Cool water should do the trick, clear her head, and snap her out of her despondent mood. She had to control her emotions or she wouldn't make it through the remaining days with him. But oh, he was so tempting   that she wished—shush up!

The gloves were off, and for her sense of pride, she had to see it through. Show him that she could survive without him, and that she didn't need him in any way. Her body ached and a quiver shot through her. She'd have to find a way to get through it, find an alternate plan.

Nineteen days left.

If anyone would be asking, begging for it, it would be him. With that pleasant thought, Ellie stepped under the spray, humming.

Twenty minutes later, dressed in her usual black leggings and hot-pink sweater with thick socks warming her feet in sneakers, she bopped into the kitchen, a plan formulating in her mind.

"Peter, I was thinking—" The kitchen was deserted. "What a

let-down." She opened the refrigerator and took out the carton of orange juice.

"What's a let-down?"

"Yikes!" She nearly jumped out of her skin, the carton almost slipping from her hand. Turning, she sucked in her breath. He stood inches from her, and she glimpsed the crinkles at the corner of his eyes, smelled the damp leather of his jacket. She leaned backward and bumped into the fridge. His warm breath fanned her cheek, tickling the sensitive spot behind her ear. His gaze shadowed, deep, intense. She wiggled. "Must you sneak up behind me?"

"I was not." He stepped to the cupboard beneath the sink and pulled out a bag of *Canine Nibbles*. "Did the let-down" – he took a couple of bone-shaped biscuits, shoved the bag back and shut the cupboard door – "have anything to do with the event upstairs?"

"I don't know what you're talking about." She sidestepped him and busied herself with finding a glass, filling it with juice, and returning the carton to the refrigerator. The frigid air smacked her face and she welcomed the cool bite, hoping it banished the heat from her flesh.

He chuckled. "Still denying, *carina*?"

"I'm denying nothing, Peter. Except that we are both adults—"

"Consenting or otherwise?"

"Stop provoking me." She shut the refrigerator door with extra force to emphasize her words.

"Am I?'

She pressed her lips together and stroked the dew forming on the outside of the glass, the action soothing her nerves. "I'm not playing, Peter"

"No?"

"Nope."

"Pity." He shrugged, and that aggravated her even more.

"I hardly think so under the circumstances," she retorted.

He shoved the dog treats in his pocket and pinned her with his dark gaze. "What is it you want, Ellie?"

There, he'd given her the opening to unload all on her mind. It seemed so easy. Yet the past five years had taught her that as simple as it appeared, that a talk should resolve their problems, sometimes the simplest things were the hardest to achieve. Her husband was no exception to this. She knew that 'telling was long past and it was showtime'. Well, she 'showed' him for two days. What of the rest? She shrugged her own query aside and, taking a sip of juice, peered at him over the rim of the glass.

"I was thinking, Peter."

He waited.

He wasn't going to make this easy, if anything, he'd make her work for everything. That was fine, because in the end she'd get what she wanted, wouldn't she? And what was that? Divorce or reconciliation? The answer dangled out of her reach.

"We have nineteen days left to spend together."

"Yes?"

She was up to something. Peter felt it in his gut. That fiasco in their bedroom earlier should have tipped him off. Instead, he misread the signals. He shook his head. When her brown eyes had shadowed with emotion and she'd given him the nod, his heart leaped into his throat, blood pulsing through him and turning him rock-hard. He'd hoped they'd settle this whole thing in bed, once and for all. But then, she dropped the bomb, *'if that's what I wanted,'* and an ice storm exploded inside him. He'd shoved her aside and flipped on his back, each breath of air, a frosty abrasion down his throat. He felt like he was ripped wide open, and his heart froze, shackling his emotions.

Now, he studied her beneath his lashes and felt a stirring in his blood. He crushed it. This time he'd be ready for her. Bide his time. She'd fall into his hands like a ripe peach—*She may do that*, the voice in his head taunted, *but no guarantee you'll be taking a bite.* Shut up. He grunted.

"Wha-at?" She cradled the glass between her palms and orange flavor wafted to him.

"Nothin'." He shook his head. "You had som'm to say?"

"Yes."

"Go ahead." He was amazed at the seemingly ordinary domestic scene they were playing out. He guffawed … there was nothing ordinary about their relationship. Turbulence had rocked them from the start and it looked like they were headed for a final clash.

He swallowed bitter taste in his mouth. Who was playing whom? And did either one of them need to pander to this ridic-ulous game? Why didn't he just grab her and do it right there on the kitchen floor? His body was primed and ready and, from what he sensed upstairs, so was hers.

He tightened his jaw against the sexual arousal. As much as he wanted her, wanted to get her out of his system, he didn't want it this way.

He wanted her to want him, crave him, ask, be—

Oh hell, what was happening between them, anyway? One thing was for sure. A man of his word, he'd see the three weeks … er … nineteen days through. Air blasted from his lungs. What condition he'd be in at the end of that time was anyone's guess.

"I thought—" She licked her lips with the tip of her tongue.

His gut jerked. "Yes?"

"—we could at least be civil to each other."

"Haven't we?" He gazed at her long and hard, noting the glass she was strangling between her hands. Did she imagine it was his neck? She bit her lip between her teeth and tapped her toe on the tile. A smile skimmed his mouth. She did that whenever she was nervous.

"Not to my liking."

"You have a preference?" he asked, arching a brow.

"Peter, must you be so difficult—"

"Me?" He advanced a step. Stopped. "Woman, if you only knew—"

"Yes?" she prompted.

Hmm, was she leading him on? Well, he was not about to be caught on a hook like a floundering seabass. "Civil, you say?"

"Mmm."

"Good idea." He leaned against the white-granite counter and folded his arms across his chest. "Exactly what I suggested two days ago."

She lifted a shapely brow and curved her lips into a smile, brightening this damp February day. His insides twisted.

"Any other changes to our living conditions?" He rubbed soreness from his jaw, the result of frequent clenching these last few days.

She circled the rim of the glass with her fingertip and then slipped it in her mouth, tasting the tartness. *Stop that, woman.* How many times had he taken her fingers in his mouth, stroking, licking, sucking with his tongue and heard her whimper with pleasure.

"No-o." A moment of confusion fleeted across her face, and she masked it by taking another sip of juice.

About to detonate, Peter expelled the pent-up air from his lungs in a harsh sound. He wanted to be anything but civil to her. Wanted to sling her over his shoulder and stride up the stairs, toss her on the bed, and beat his chest like Tarzan, the conqueror. *Take a cold shower, Medeci.* He was not of the Stone Age, but a twenty-first-century man who had to curb his ardor in the guise of civil behavior. A wistful twist to his mouth. Even though she put him through hell, it didn't stop him from imagining this woman he married, under him, fused with him, one with him, riding him to the heights of sexual fulfillment.

He cleared his throat. "Only fair that I make a suggestion too, don't you think?"

Suspicion settled on her every feature.

"I was about to take King for a walk."

Her eyes grew wide. She stepped away from him, and the kitchen counter pressed into her back.

"I'd like you to come with me." If he could get them on a friendly footing, get her to talk with him, open up to him again, he'd get what he wanted at the end of this interlude, one way or another. And what was that? Divorce or reconciliation? The answer eluded him. He tautened his jaw, banishing the question.

"Go fly a kite, Doc." She plunked the glass in the sink with force and juice splashed onto her hand. "And take that beast with you." She raised her hand and licked tangy liquid from her fingers with the tip of her tongue.

He groaned, blood surging to a major part of his male anatomy and making him throb. He took a step toward her, then checked himself, controlling his lust. Didn't take much for her to turn him on. Every muscle in his body tensed, and he gulped down his frustration. "Afraid?"

She hesitated, her face reflecting her inner struggle. "Yes." She wiped her sticky hand on her thigh.

"I bet when you get to know King, fear will fly out the window."

"Uh, uh."

"Are you game?" It was a challenge and she wouldn't turn it down, especially issued by him. He inhaled a breath, exhaled, the sound rough even to his own ears. Except she resisted his overtures in the bedroom—and that irked him big time. He frowned. Had he missed a clue?

"What's the bet?"

His frown dissolved into a smile. She was on the brink of capitulating. "If I'm right," he said, thinking how to best phrase his words so she wouldn't bolt. Heck, the best defense was an offense. "Have dinner with me."

"You're asking me for a date?" She laughed in disbelief. "After nearly five years, you're asking?"

"Yeah." Must he grovel? Had it been that long since they had an evening out alone? She had always seemed busy with her circle of friends—a niggling thought—or had they been his social circle, and his business dinners they attended? He gulped down a self-deprecating guffaw. Then, he set his jaw. She had seemed friendly enough with Louie at the club. He expelled a harsh breath. Indeed, time had swept by, and a date with just the two of them was what the doctor ordered. And with the end result he determined to have.

"And if you're wrong?"

"You set the stakes." He unfolded his arms and rubbed his chin with the back of his hand. *Dangerous, Doc.* He was treading a tightrope, playing into her hand like that, but he figured it was well worth the risk.

"Sure?"

He didn't like the way she said that, tilting her head and squinting at him. She was about to toss him another grenade. He sensed it in his gut and prepped for it. "Yeah."

"I leave in three days."

Silence filled the room. Tension vibrated around them, pressuring.

"If I'm wrong" – he played his ace – "I'll drive you wherever you want to go."

"Even back to the club?"

He narrowed his focus. "Mmm."

"And how'd that look for the election?"

He shrugged. "Shouldn't make much difference by then."

"I-I see." Her words were so quiet that he strained to hear. "Deal?"

Chapter 9

Fear snaked through her at the sight of the dog. She felt silly, a grown woman, being so afraid of a puppy. But he was a big puppy.

"You want to hold the leash for a while?" Peter asked.

"No, thanks." After days of procrastination, she agreed to go on this walk, but kept her distance from man and beast. Both were dangerous. The dog reminded her of the terrifying event in her childhood, and the man, of his overpowering personality that had nearly swamped her.

King barked and she jumped another foot away. "We did agree to keep this a short walk, didn't we, Peter?"

Amazement glimmered in his eyes. "It's only been five minutes, Ellie." He strolled a few paces ahead. "Give it another fifteen at least."

She glanced at her wristwatch. "Not a moment longer." A bead of sweat slid between her breasts. She collapsed on a boulder beside the trail in Malibu Canyon Park and watched them. Man and beast exemplified strength, power, and physical fitness. Rugged, beautiful—untamed.

Breath stalled in her chest, her pulse vibrated, her palms damp.

Peter picked up a stick and threw it. The dog chased after it, retrieved it, and raced back to him, tail wagging. Laughing, Peter rubbed the dog's ears. "Good boy."

When they set out for the outing, Ellie had scrambled onto the back seat of the Mercedes, to see the beast better. No way would she sit in the front and have the Doberman breathing down her neck from behind. She would've freaked out for sure. And she wouldn't give Peter the satisfaction of watching her do so.

Peter had thrown an old blanket over the front seat and the dog bounded in, barking excitedly. A satisfied smile settled on her mouth. From her vantage point, she had them both in her sights.

Ellie breathed in the scents of nature. At this higher elevation, air was pure, crisp and fresh, a soothing balm to her rattled nerves. Another twig whirled through the air and King caught it in his teeth. Hair on the back of her neck stood on end. The dog bypassed Peter and dropped his prize at her feet. She draped her arms around her bended knees and shrank back on her perch. The animal stared at her with his luminous eyes, tongue lolling and tail wagging. He barked. She whimpered.

"He likes you," Peter said.

She shook her head, too numb to speak.

"Come 'ere boy."

The dog hesitated, perplexed at her reaction and trotted back to Peter.

"He was being friendly, Ellie." Peter rubbed the dog's neck. "Wanted to play with you."

"No-o, thank you." She waved them on, air whizzing between her teeth.

"You coming or not?" Peter called to her while King investigated a maple trunk. "If you don't, you'll forfeit the wager."

"No way." She may not want to keep company with either man or beast, but she wouldn't forfeit the bet and the sense of control that came with winning. Slapping her hands on her thighs, she stood and marched right passed them.

Ellie kept on walking until she was several feet ahead of them, then screwed up her face. Peter had been quick to agree to her leaving prior to three weeks if the wager went her way. Was he tired of her already? Did he want to appease his conscience with this interval? Say, he had tried to save his marriage to gain empathy?

The Board elections would be over by then and having served her purpose as the 'good doctor's wife' for this round of political power plays, he'd have no further need of her. She tilted her chin. Well, she had her own agenda; rerouting her life on a new and exciting direction.

No doubt, Peter would secure the Chairmanship. Might not be an easy task, but he welcomed the challenge. Relentless in his pursuit of what he wanted, he succeeded. Wasn't that why he chased after her and brought her back, for appearances sake to cover all his bases?

She'd make his success work for her too, and leave with her conscience clear to pursue her dream. A stitch at her side warned that it might not be as simple as she imagined. She shrugged it off.

First thing would be to call Louie, get herself reinstated in *The Blue Room,* and go from there. That could be in just three days if she came out on top with this bet. Tremors ran through her. Was it excitement or dread?

Pondering her own query, Ellie strolled to the shoulder of the trail and peered over the pine trees at the Pacific Ocean in the distance. "This is a priceless view of Malibu Beach."

"Yeah," Peter said, staring at her. Her leggings were molded to her legs, her sweater hugged her derriere and a sunbeam glinted off the crown of her head. A raw, primitive urge shot through him. He wanted to stomp behind her, cup her with his hands and nuzzle her nape with his mouth, his tongue … He feigned a cough. "Ellie, watch your step."

"Hey, a sailboat." She stood on tiptoe and pointed toward the horizon. "Looks like a toy from up here."

"You're too close to the edge." He strode nearer. "It might—"

The earth caved beneath her feet and she screamed.

"Ellie!" Peter dived for her but King rammed him aside, leaped up and knocked her back onto solid ground.

"Wha-at happened?" Shaken, she snapped her lashes open and stared into the dog's golden-brown eyes. King had her pinned to the ground, his paws on her chest, growling his reprimand. She shut her eyes, and a shrill sound erupted from her lungs, echoing in the wooded glen.

"Good, boy." Peter seized the dog by the collar and pulled him off her. Grabbing her hand, he hauled her to her feet, and the abrupt motion slammed her hard against his chest.

She clutched his shoulders, tears of relief brimming on her lashes.

"King saved you from a serious tumble over the cliff." The thought of what nearly happened and with him not two feet from her, cut into him like a scalpel. He sucked in a breath and gripped her shoulders. "You nearly gave me a heart—" The remainder of his words lodged in his throat, his mouth on hers, the adrenaline rush fueling him.

He tasted her sweetness and her fear. When she whimpered, he soothed with his tongue. Slow strokes inside her mouth over and over until he sensed panic dissipate and desire flare. He deepened the kiss, his lips more demanding. She sighed into his mouth and slid her tongue over his, initiating another erotic duel.

His heart pumped blood at record speed. He was hot, he was sweaty, and he was aroused. He'd be taking her smack in the middle of the trail if he didn't put the brakes on. A fevered moment and he tore his mouth away from hers, pressed her head to his shoulder, and brushed her hair with a slightly unsteady hand.

Ellie remained in his embrace until her breathing regulated. When she did pull away, she brushed her moist palms on her thighs, and King slurped at her knuckles. She jumped and a cry burst from her.

"He's giving you a kiss too, glad you're okay." Peter rifled in his pocket for a biscuit and handed it to her. "Give it to him, a thank you."

She remained immobile. "You give it to him."

"No can do."

The Doberman watched her and with his tongue hanging out, waited. A tense moment, and Peter slapped the biscuit in her hand. "Give."

She licked her lips, gulped down her nervousness, and after a hesitant moment, offered the treat to the dog. King took a tentative step closer, and then another, and she quickly tossed it to him. "Thank you, dog."

"King."

"King."

The dog wolfed down the biscuit and lifted his head, waiting for another.

"Name suits him," she said.

"Yes."

Peter put another biscuit in her hand and, without thinking, she extended it to the dog. The animal jumped for it and without touching her fingers, crunched it.

A nervous giggle slid off her tongue. "He carries himself like royalty." She glanced at her husband and a faint smile tugged at her mouth. "Like his owner."

Peter grinned. "Don't know what you're talking 'bout, woman." He guided her back to the Mercedes with the dog loping between them. "You've made a friend for life."

Ellie faltered in her step. "So, I have." And realized, in doing so, she'd lost the bet. She pressed her fingers upon her lips still tingling from his kiss, a reminder that his heat had speared through her fear. She trembled at the thought of what might have happened if King hadn't knocked her to safety. A sliver of apprehension lingered, but it was the sexual tension vibrating between her and Peter that made her snatch her breath.

In that brief moment in his arms, she tasted his passion and something else. His own fear? Uncertainty? Anger? Whichever it was, it meant Peter wasn't as indifferent to her as he made out. Her feather-light smile turned into a satisfied grin.

Peter was settling the brute in the front seat, and she peered at him from beneath her lashes.

That little bit of sensual knowledge could come in handy in the days to follow. *Huh! you were like a ripe plum in his hands, girlie,* the voice in her head taunted. *If he hadn't rammed the brakes on that kiss, you'd be rolling on the grass beneath that poplar, half undressed*—Hardly! But deep inside her, she knew it to be true and blushed.

In a huff, she flounced in the back seat of the auto. Okay, this round went to him, but it was by no means over. She'd yet have him eating out of her hand. A satisfied sound gurgled from her throat, and Peter raised an eyebrow at her. "I'll look forward to our ... er ... dinner date, Peter."

"An event to remember."

"Will it be?" she asked.

He winked. "I'll make sure of it." He shut the door and sauntered to the driver's seat, a smug look on his face.

Peter—the distinguished neurosurgeon, smug?

Her pulse leaped, and she bit her lip. Definitely, she'd have to rethink her strategy.

Chapter 10

"That was lovely," Ellie said, setting the fork on her near-empty plate.

"Best chicken in *salsa al vino* here." Peter smiled, pushing back his plate.

"I remember." She blotted her mouth with the linen napkin.

"You do?" He picked up his wine glass and sipped, his eyes steady on her face, wondering what she was thinking about him ... about them.

Earlier that evening, she'd glided down the stairs in that sexy number of a dress, the neckline dipping to the swell of her breasts, the deep-blue fabric hugging her curvy bod. The silk flowed down her legs and flared at her feet, skimming her matching pumps. When she paused by the chandelier in the foyer, light glimmered on her shoulders and made her hair shine.

He'd manhandled the back of a chair to stop from stepping up, slinging her over his shoulder, and heading back upstairs, dinner forgotten in lieu of the dessert in front of him. He grinned. The material tucked at her waistline made her appear so tiny, he figured he could span her with his hands. Then, he drew his brows over the bridge of his nose; or had she lost weight without him realizing it?

"Yes." She fingered the checkered napkin in her lap, before patting it smooth. "Can't you tell?" She chuckled, pointing to her plate.

"Glad you enjoyed it." Man, he was fumbling for words like a teenager out on his first date.

"I guess I was hungrier than I thought."

"Good." Not as hungry as I'm feeling, he thought, taking in her luscious appearance.

"All that exercise—"

"Yeah." He watched her over the rim of his wine glass. Her hair was swept up in a type of knot at the nape of her neck—it was beyond him how she'd managed to fasten it like that. A few wisps caressed her temples. If he leaned in just a few inches to whisper in her ear, he'd feel silk across his lips and smell the scent of her shampoo.

He raised the goblet to his mouth. She brushed a loose curl behind her ear and bumped the sapphire earring dangling from her earlobe. Elegant plus. His temperature was rising. Images of action moves they could indulge in after dinner flooded his mind. He gulped down the remainder of his drink and set the glass on the table. "Dance?"

The Italian bistro's dance floor was filling up. A melody beckoned and Ellie glanced about her. Attentive waiters in tight-fitting black-and- white uniforms flitted between candle-lit tables. The mural across one wall depicted Venice gondoliers serenading couples touring the famed canals of the magical city. Ambiance— the ultimate in romance.

For Ellie, the intimate setting spelled danger. It was here at the *Cucina Italiano* that Peter had proposed to her five years ago. Reliving the past wouldn't help with the future she was after. She felt a pang, but shrugged it off. To conquer it, she had to confront it.

"Yes." She set her napkin on the small table and pinned a smile on her lips. It could be their last dance. The pang cut deep. She ignored it.

Peter pushed his chair back and, taking her hand, pulled her to her feet. Her eyes collided with his. High voltage crackled between them. She could hardly breathe. He stroked his thumb along the curve of her cheek and then guided her onto the floor.

She melted in his arms, her head upon his shoulder, the fabric of his jacket rough beneath her cheek. His touch unleashed fantasies she'd kept bound up inside her for the past three months. She swayed with him to the sensuous rhythm, imagining how wonderful this would be if it were real.

This was a stolen moment. She'd be smart to remember that.

The song seduced. For these few minutes, she'd pretend he was her Prince Charming and she his princess ... he was her knight in shining armor, her champion, and she his lady. Behind his back she curled her fingers in a fist. Not the driven man who'd risen to the top and wasn't about to let up, even at the dissolution of their marriage. Her nails dug into her palms. How high was the top for Peter? She opened her hands and spanned his back, feeling his strength beneath her fingers. For tonight, she'd pretend he was not the ruthless, cunning man who'd become her provider and she his prize.

Peter brushed his lips across her temple and acute sensation tingled through her. She reached up and caressed the nape of his neck, his heat a catalyst to emotion surging inside her. For this one night, Ellie danced with the man of her dreams.

Having forgone a tie, he was dressed in navy slacks, his white shirt beneath his jacket unbuttoned halfway to his waist. Dark hair sprang from his chest. She was tempted to slide her hand inside, follow with her mouth to kiss, taste, lick. She missed her footing and fumbled the step.

"Steady there," he murmured in her ear. His breath laced with a hint of wine, teased the sensitive area, scrambling her insides.

She nodded, unable to utter a word, for fear it'd give her reaction to him away. Prickles of awareness shot through her and—

A riotous couple jostled them and Ellie's fantasy splintered. The band played the final note on a crescendo, followed by a millisecond of silence, and then applause erupted around them.

"Thank you, Peter."

"My pleasure." He kept his hand on the small of her back and escorted her back to their table. "What say we have coffee at home?"

"Yes," she said, glad to get away from the romantic atmosphere.

While Peter paid the bill and retrieved her wrap, Ellie gripped her evening bag so tight the sequins imprinted marks on her fingertips. She cast him a surreptitious glance. Why had he chosen to bring her here? Was it to show her that memories didn't move him? Or to signal they'd come full circle and time for closure of their life, their marriage?

"Will you be warm enough in this?" He placed the light wrap across her shoulders, his fingers feathering the nape of her neck.

A quiver shot through her and fine down on the back of her neck stood on end. "Ye-es, thanks." She placed her hand on the crook of his arm and they strolled outside just as the valet drove up with the Mercedes.

* * *

After Peter had lit the fireplace in the den, he tossed his jacket on the sofa, rolled up his sleeves, and manned the bar. "Café mocha with a dash of Kahlua?"

"Mmm, a very small dash." She needed her wits about her. Chemistry between them had always been magnetic and tonight she felt caught in the force field of that attraction.

He chuckled. "Just the way you like it."

"With whipped cream and oodles of chocolate sprinkles." She laughed and wondered if he could hear the slight strain in her voice.

Memories flashed through her mind of earlier, happier times together.

"You bet."

"Yum."

He pressed the button on the blender and the whirring sound suffocated his next words. "Yum is right, *mia bella*." Flipping two crystal glasses into his palms from the shelf beneath the counter, he set them on top and filled them with chocolate liquid.

"Smells heavenly."

"Heaven it will be, *cara mia*." He squirted an extra blob of whipping cream on hers and showered it with chocolate shavings.

Her head shot up at his words. Was he up to something? Her mind seemed fuzzy. Not from wine, she rarely imbibed, but from the warmth of the room and the feeling of wellbeing permeating through her. Questions struggled to get through this lull in her thinking, but she kept them at bay. Flames in the grate tantalized and she stepped closer. Somehow, she managed to curl down on the carpet; a difficult feat in her tight-fitting dress.

"Here you are, *principessa*." Peter offered her the cocktail and adjusting his pant leg slightly, lowered himself down beside her. "Just the way you like it." He bent one knee, rested his arm on it, and held his cup with his other hand.

Ellie cradled the cup between her palms, warmth soothing her hands and rich cocoa flavor tempting her. She raised it to her lips, licked whipping cream with the tip of her tongue and felt like she was tasting the forbidden.

She chanced a glance at Peter before her eyelids dipped to half-mast. Testosterone seemed to ooze from his every pore. A pocket of air wedged in her throat and a bead of moisture trickled between her breasts. He'd pampered her, especially after a night of sensual pleasures. In the morning, she found some bauble, some trinket on her pillow. He showered her with such a wealth of gifts she'd begun to feel more like a kept woman than his wife.

Chocolate flavor in her mouth turned bittersweet.

Ellie yearned to be a wife in every sense of the word and not just in bed. But Peter's demanding work schedule left him so exhausted that when he came home, all he wanted to do was play … with her … and leave the world beyond the mansion out.

She had become so isolated in her gilded castle that when Peter globetrotted to symposiums expostulating the wonders of medical science, she felt like the fairytale princess locked up in her palace. But for Ellie, the Prince didn't come to her rescue, he was the one unwittingly imprisoning her.

Her mouth drooped at the corners. Although he telephoned her, it was always on the run between engagements. From every place he traveled, he sent her a present, two, ten … when all she wanted was him; to be a part of his life and share her life, her dreams with him.

She reclined against the arm of the sofa and stretched her legs in front of her on the thick carpet. Thoughts of what might have been mocked, and she pushed them far back in her mind. If all she had with her husband was this one night, then she'd take it. Add it to her collection of memorabilia. A tremulous smile flitted across her lips. She raised the goblet to her mouth and took another sip of the sweet concoction.

"Mmm, this is tastier than I thought." She licked white froth from her top lip with the tip of her tongue. "It's really good."

"Let me." Peter set his drink on the floor, then took hers and placed it beside his.

"I can do—"

"You missed a spot." Peter flicked cream from her mouth with his fingertip and placed it in his mouth. "Mmm, sweet."

"Yes," she breathed, a shallow sound.

"Ellie." He leaned closer and his words fanned her cheek, his chocolate-laced breath tantalizing her mouth. Flicking his tongue out, he licked the remaining cream from her lip. "I want some more."

She swallowed the lump in her throat. "Me-e, too."

In a millisecond, he plundered her mouth, his tongue gliding over hers, initiating a seductive tango in her mouth. She matched his fervor and tasted passion, vulnerability, longing.

"Ellie," he breathed into her mouth.

"Peter, my l—"

He smothered her declaration with his lips and gently pushed her on the carpet, half lying on top of her. She wrapped her arms around his neck and, drawing him closer, swept her fingers through his hair.

He trailed his hand across the curve of her bare shoulder, along her collarbone, his thumb caressing the pulse point at her throat. Every spot his fingers stroked, he followed with his mouth, finally settling on her cleavage. He slid the blue silk down her arms, until her breasts filled his palms. Groaning he lowered his head, grazing the nipple with his teeth. A purr worked its way up from deep in her throat. He stroked her other breast with slightly trembling fingers until her nipple puckered. Then, he switched and drew it fully into his mouth, suckling … sweet torture.

Holding him close, Ellie spanned her hands across his back and around until she found her way beneath his shirt. Her fingers slid across his torso, outlining every muscle, every curve and crevice.

Peter lifted his head and pillaged her mouth with his tongue. A sound of utter pleasure dropped from her lips and onto his. Skimming his hand beneath her breasts, Peter set her abdomen fluttering. His fingers glided over the curve of her hip to her thigh and further, exploring the shape of a long, slender leg. He pushed the hem of her dress upward and feathering her foot with his fingertips, discarded her high-heeled pump. He brushed her instep and sensation shot through her nerves. He stoked the blaze between them … his hand upon her calf, pushing silk fabric higher, he stroked her inner thigh, each brush of his fingers inching closer to her moist center.

A burning log in the fire grate crackled, a backdrop to their breathing.

Ellie moved beneath him, thinking she'd die of need, anticipation, desire. "Peter, my dea—"

"Ellie, *cara*—"

Ring! Ring!

The sudden ringing of the doorbell jolted them. Peter's words froze on his lips and Ellie stilled in his embrace.

"No-o." Peter pressed his forehead into her bosom, willing the intruder to go away.

She caressed his hair with her fingertips. She inhaled a deep puff of oxygen and her breasts lifted, brushing his face. His sharp intake of breath mingled with hers. Through the silk of her dress, his steel length pressed into the apex of her thighs. She wanted him … wanted to feel him inside her, and the future, be that what it may. A suspended moment, and common sense fought through her tumultuous feelings. "Pet-er."

The bell peeled a third time, insistent.

"It might be important." She forced the words from deep in her throat and wriggled from beneath him. Air hit her moist flesh and she shivered.

"Do not move," he huffed, still holding onto her.

Peter heaved a deep breath and, about to explode, exhaled a miniature hurricane. He'd waited so long for her, to touch her, to have her. Other nights he would not think of. Tonight was his with her and he wouldn't relinquish it. Nothing could be more important than this. The crossroads of his marriage, his life, and his future with this woman he'd married. He grazed her cheek with his knuckles and then kissed her long and hard. At last, he dragged himself up and tossed a stray lock of hair off his brow. He remained fixed to the spot, staring down at her, sexual energy like a livewire between them.

Ellie lounged on the carpet—his woman, his wife. Her dress pooled at her waist, her hair mussed, her lips slightly swollen from his kisses, her breasts straining for his caress. He moved to touch her, fondle, taste her again, then, checking the motion, stuffed his hand in his pocket.

"Whoever's out there better send up a flare." He was in no mood to be civil, especially when Ellie began straightening her dress and slipping on her shoes. "Who the heck could be calling at midnight?" He shoved his shirt in his waistband and stomped to the door, his tongue skimming his mouth. Her taste lingered on his lips and his gut jerked … he craved more of her. He yanked the door open and a laugh teased, but a scowl won out.

"Good evening, *senor*."

"Good night is what you mean." He opened his mouth to say something more, and then clamped it shut before he blurted something he'd later regret. His housekeeper pushed passed him, her arms loaded with packages. "What are you doing here, Marta?"

"I've brought you food." She flashed her dark eyes up at him and in her no-nonsense manner, marched toward the kitchen. "*Lasagna, enchiladas* and your favorite Mexican sweet bread."

He rubbed his cheek. "Couldn't we do this tomorrow?"

He didn't want food. He wanted Ellie, who was in the den getting dressed. Frustration gnawed at his insides.

"No." She turned and, to his utter amazement, her face crumpled, tears rolling down her cheeks.

"What's the matter?" His hand hovered over her shoulder and then he gave her an awkward pat, not sure how to handle an emotional woman at a time like this. "Can I help you?"

She sniffed, shaking her head, and caught a glimpse of Ellie in the other room. "*Buenas noches, Senora Medeci*." She jostled containers in her arms and swiped at her cheeks with her sleeve. Before Ellie could respond, she plunked the packages in Peter's arms. "Am leaving for Mexico … the husband of my sister … he leave her for *chola*."

Peter crinkled his brow. "*Chola*?"

Marta screwed up her face like a mutinous prune and continued without answering him. "I go find him. Knock his brains out." She proceeded to illustrate by making a fist and hitting her forehead.

"Easy now."

She laughed, and then hiccupped. Her oversized bosom heaved and nearly tipped her petite, plump body over. She waved her agitated hands around. "*Chola, senor*. Loose woman, 'ho, street girl."

"Uh huh." Peter nodded and wisely refrained from further comment.

"I go now."

Yes, please, he thought. Marta's sister's woes were not what he needed to hear now, considering he teetered on his own marital seesaw.

"Good luck." From the corner of his eye, he glimpsed Ellie edging toward the door. He couldn't let his chance just drift away before he … she … they—

"Thank you, *senor*," Marta said in her accented English, interrupting his sensual thoughts.

"Welcome," he muttered, ushering her to the front door. Suddenly, she stopped and he almost bumped into her, and it was all he could do to keep the casseroles from spilling a new color scheme on the Persian carpet.

"I didn't want to use the back-door key. Maybe someone think I'm thief. I saw light and—"

"I understand." He edged toward the open door, hoping she'd get the message. "*Bon voyage*."

"What you say?"

"*Bon*—never mind." A half-smile skipped across his lips. "Have a good trip."

She opened her arms wide and hugged him, food and all. "You are like my own son." She gave him a smacking kiss on his cheek

111

and waddled out to the dinged-up Corolla, motioning to the morose man behind the wheel.

Soon as she slid in the passenger seat, he revved up the motor and drove off.

"*Buenas noches,*" Marta yelled, leaning far out the window.

"Goodnight." Peter shut the door with the back of his foot and turned to Ellie, feeling anything but the suave physician.

"You need help with those?" she asked.

"Na-a. I'll just put them—"

"Then, I'll say goo-oodnight."

"Ellie," he murmured, stepping closer. Balancing the dishes against his chest, he was tempted to chuck them over his shoulder and grab her, continuing where they left off. She under him, his mouth on hers, his hand on her—

"I had a lovely time, Peter." She drew nearer, and he held his breath. Then, she leaned into him and kissed his cheek.

His cheek. Like he was old faithful or some such fellow by her side, when only moments ago fireworks ... heck, megaworks were about to explode between them. He gulped down his disappointment, watching her turn and glide up the stairs to—their bedroom, he hoped.

Emptiness gnawed in his gut. He almost had her, had what he dreamed about, desired, craved these months. A heavy sigh lumbered out from deep inside him. He knew the seduction scene was over. If he made a play for her now, he'd lose in the blink of an eye. And she'd come out the winner. He stalked to the kitchen, every muscle in his body tense.

Upstairs in her bedroom, Ellie removed her earrings, thankful for Marta's timely interruption. And if she hadn't felt so embarrassed by nearly being caught in a state of *dishabille* by the housekeeper, she would have found the whole thing comical. Especially with Peter standing under the chandelier with his arms laden with delicious-smelling dishes.

At the moment, Ellie couldn't even work up a smile. Her body buzzed with unfulfilled desire, nerve endings stimulated, heart throbbing. If Marta had delayed five minutes, she knew from her fevered response to him, she would have fallen right into his hand.

Heat suffused her face. What had she almost done? It would've been a disaster. She slipped the shoes from her feet and wriggled from her gown. Would it have been so bad to indulge in a romantic evening with her husband? She glanced up and caught her reflection in the mirror. Her breasts still glowed from his touch, the nipples puckering. She groaned and brushing her fingers over them, she splayed her hand across her abdomen, bringing it to rest on the curve of her hip.

A moan of such need erupted from the center of her being that she quickly turned away from her reflection. She picked up her dress off the floor, walked to the closet and hung it up. Busy. Keep busy, she reminded herself. Shoes were placed in their spot. She stepped to the bed, pulled her nightie from behind the pillow, and slipped into it. After she fluffed the pillows, she slumped on the edge of the bed.

What had she expected—a night of unreserved declarations? A sigh tore from her. His agenda hadn't changed, and now that she had one of her own, they were butting heads ... possibly all the way to the divorce court.

She swallowed the bitter taste in her mouth.

If she imagined a night of lovemaking would change anything, she'd be greatly mistaken. He'd follow his course of action as usual, thinking it was all right with her. Any progress she made by challenging him and setting her own terms to their three-week liaison would lose impact. She raised her head, removed pins from her hair and shook it loose over her shoulders. She'd get over it ... him. *Think again, my girl.* "Oh, be quiet." She tossed the pins on the dresser and slipped under the covers.

She'd use the bathroom later, long after he finished, thus avoiding another encounter with him tonight. She pulled the blankets up to her chin and replayed the fantasy evening in her mind. Moistness pressed against her lashes and a lone tear slipped out, rolling down her cheek.

Downstairs, Peter shoved packages in the freezer with such force, he could've strangled someone. Air exploded from him, frosting in the icy compartment. He'd been so close, so close to her, so close to having her, so close to having her admit, so close to having answers to questions that battered his mind, so close— *You didn't score, Doc.* Shut up, brain.

Iciness of the freezer cooled his feverish flesh. He still felt her beneath his hands, her smooth skin, the taste of her mouth, sweet like strawberry wine, her scent … And her moan of sheer delight had been his near-defeat. He glanced at his crotch and, sure enough, his need was making itself known. He placed a hand there, adjusted the material of his trousers and breathed easier, but not much.

He slammed the freezer shut, turned the light off, and marched from the kitchen, wondering why she rushed away from him. She'd been responding to him. After Marta left, she avoided further physical contact with him. But why had she kissed him? A tease? Of what he tasted but didn't get? Had he underestimated her? Was she playing her own seductive game, and was he the prey? His heart booted back in protest. His mind mocked. *Why not? Wasn't that what you're doing?* But that's because he wanted her to take him at face value, to trust him, believe in him, no questions asked. *To teach her a lesson, just a little one. Maybe there's a lesson in this for you, Doc.* He laughed, loud and hard, the sound bouncing off the foyer walls.

A moment later, he sobered. *Get a handle, man.* He'd been behaving like a tongue-tied schoolboy receiving his first kiss. His marriage was disintegrating before his eyes, and he didn't know how to stop it. If he were honest, he'd admit he was clutching at straws.

He was either going to have her or let her go. A rush of such agony filled him that he buckled over and pounded the banister with his fist. He heaved a deep breath and it hissed out between his teeth.

Okay, Mrs. Medeci. A flash of a smile. She still carried his name. His smile vanished. This round went to her. He drew his lips in a taut line and climbed the steps to his bedroom, one thought sustaining him. There'd be another round ... a final round. "Winner take all." And he intended to take the victory.

Chapter 11

At eight o'clock the next morning Ellie trudged down the stairs, yawning. Groggy from her restless night, she grabbed onto the banister to avoid stumbling, thoughts zigzagging in her brain.

"G' mornin', wife." Peter trotted past, slinging on his jacket and almost knocking her over.

"Goo-od morning." She swung around and tightened her grip on the railing, glad she'd reached the bottom step.

"Emergency." He hurried in and out of his office in two seconds flat and, with his briefcase under his arm, yanked the front door open. A minuscule pause, and he glanced at her like he was about to say something more but changed his mind. "See you later." He slammed the door behind him, the sound reverberating around her.

"Some vacation time," Ellie murmured, but he was already gone. Although dressed in her customary black leggings and a ruby-red pullover that reached to mid-thigh, chills had her rubbing her hands over her arms.

Once again, the day stretched ahead of her, empty until Peter returned home. Her stomach stitched. When would he be home? She shook her head, trying to unravel her feelings and find her purpose in this marriage. The bittersweet events of last night flashed through her mind and, not wanting to dwell on them, she hurried past the den. She paused by the foyer window and glanced up at the sky.

A ray of sunshine pierced through the clouds. A good sign? She chuckled at her foolishness. A lonesome howl cut through the stillness and fear snaked through her. When it sounded again, she swallowed her nervousness and squared her shoulders. A brisk walk around the grounds might help clear her mind.

She toured the gazebo behind the house, scent of jasmine wafting to her from its trellis-like frame. The perfume reminded her of her wedding to Peter and a lump of emotion rose in her throat. How had they come from that idyllic day to the brink of divorce today?

She marched across the lawn, her boots squelching on the dew-drenched grass, until she came to the little bridge that had always enchanted her. Clambering across, she paused and leaned over the railing to glimpse goldfish swimming in the pond beneath. A sigh, and she glanced up at a bluebird in flight.

Over the years, Peter had soared to the heights of his professional journey, but she had yet to begin hers. Something she intended to change at the end of this interim period.

Her desire to make their marriage work battled with her desire to fulfill other needs in her life. This last lap of the three weeks should zip by, and she'd have her answer. In winning her life back, would she lose Peter? And if she didn't, would she lose herself all over again?

She stomped over the bridge, stepped off, and stumbled in her footing. Snatching up the stone beneath her boot, she hurled it across the green.

King barked.

She jumped, seeing him not three yards from her. The beast lay in his doghouse with a morose look in his eyes. A moment of indecision kept her fixed to the spot, and then she swung away.

He whined and she paused. Another whimper tugged at her heart. She turned around and took a pace nearer.

"What's the matter, boy?" Emboldened by his sad countenance, she stepped closer, yet maintaining a safe distance.

The Doberman raised his head a fraction for a better look and then flopped it back down between his paws.

"You're hungry." She noted his empty bowl and rubbed her hands together for courage. "Peter forgot to feed you, rushing out like he did."

The dog looked at her with his doleful eyes. What was she to do? A twinge of guilt stabbed her at the thought of the dog going hungry. Peter wouldn't be back for hours. "You sensed that, did you?"

A soft woof.

"You miss him, too."

Her heart thudded. A quick breath and she snatched his food and water tray, imagining he'd snap her fingers off. When he didn't, pent-up air whooshed from deep in her chest and she chuckled in nervous relief. She hurried away, his bark following her. After she'd gone several steps along the cobblestone path, she tossed over her shoulder. "I'll be back, dog."

It took her five minutes to wash the containers, fill one with doggy pellets and the other with fresh water. Another minute brought her to King's door with her knees knocking. The dog hadn't moved.

"I know how you feel." She set the food in front of him and leaped back. "You must eat, boy. Keep up your strength."

The dog quirked an ear, liking the sound of her voice and her attention. Getting up, he stretched, and without giving her another glance, sampled the fare.

"Must taste good, you ol' pooch." She settled on the grass and watched him wolf it down. "Ignoring me like that."

King finished his chow and gave a pleased bark.

"Amazing what a nice meal will do for the disposition, hey?"

The beast answered with two consecutive woofs.

"Wish I could activate my appetite as quickly." She stood, brushed at her bottom to dislodge grass sticking to her sweater and turned to go. "S' long."

King protested her leaving with incessant barking.

"What now?"

He walked toward her and she backed off. He paced away, then forward again, wagging his tail.

"Oh, no." She shook her finger at him. "You'll have to wait for Peter for that."

King yelped, and she laughed. "You do know how to twist me around your little paw, don't you?" She took several steps closer. "Som'm you learned from Peter?" A trembling breath eased between her lips. "Tsk, tsk, and you and I are just getting to know each other." Unhooking the leash from the wall, she paused, her stomach tensing. What if he bit her? She gulped down her uneasiness and clicked the strap onto his collar.

"Come on then." Her hands were clammy and she held on tight. "Where to, my friend?"

Several hours later, Ellie stood in the kitchen, blotting moisture from her brow with her sleeve and wondering who had flashed a camera at them, then hurried down the street. It had been the moment she'd paid the street vendor for the hotdog and bottle of water. Shaking her head, she took a soda from the refrigerator, slammed the door shut, and dismissed the incident.

Humming a tune, she opened the can, and the carbonated liquid fizzed. She raised the soda to her mouth and the phone rang. A giggle teased her lips. She lifted the cordless from the counter, plunked down on a chair, and propped her foot on her knee. "Hello."

"Ellie."

Her heart flipped and her foot hit the floor. "Yes."

A beat of silence.

"I won't be home until very late, if at all, tonight."

A quiet moment from her end.

"King needs to be fed."

"Done."

"Who?"

"You won the bet, remember?"

He laughed, but it sounded half-hearted through the airwaves. "Yeah."

She set the soda can on the table and outlined the Pepsi logo with her index finger. "He took me for a walk."

"Hmm," he said. "Infringing on my territory."

"What d' you mean?" She curled her fingers around the can, condensation dampening her palm.

He started to say something and she held her breath. "Had fun?"

She sighed her disappointment, but he couldn't hear that. "Yes." She fidgeted on the chair. "He missed you."

"And have you missed me, too, Ellie?"

Loaded seconds plodded by.

"Guess that answers my question," he murmured, background noises crackling through the line. "Gotta go."

"Peter, I-I—" but the dial tone droned in her ear.

She replaced the receiver. She should have asked him about the emergency. Should have answered his question, 'have you missed me?' But she couldn't. Not just yet.

Was he playing with her emotions? Have her so emotionally dependent that she'd feel a helpless damsel who had to rely on him for her survival? She balked at the thought and hurried from the kitchen, soda can forgotten on the table. She refused to behave like she had no mind or life of her own apart from her husband. And there lay her dilemma.

She ran into the den to find solace and stopped short. The curtains were closed and ashes remained in the grate, the gloomy atmosphere reflecting her life. She shrugged the notion away and grabbed the afghan, a wedding gift from Peter's mother, off the back of the sofa. Kicking off her boots, she flung herself on the couch and, drawing the covering close to her chin, snuggled in the warmth. Images of last night replayed in her mind. She punched a cushion and turned over on her tummy. After an hour of tossing and turning, Ellie closed her eyes and drifted off to sleep.

* * *

Peter drove along the circular path to the veranda and turned off the ignition. Rubbing the sting from his eyes, he squinted at the digital clock on the dashboard. Three a.m. Every muscle in his body ached, and he leaned back against the plush upholstery for a moment.

When he'd rushed to the hospital, he expected a routine surgery and was confronted with a tug-o-war with life and death. Hospital bureaucracy compounded the situation, and he'd been ready to blow a fuse at the mumbo jumbo causing a delay. Seconds counted in saving the boy's life.

Already pegged a rebel doc in the hospital wards for his unconventional bedside manner, he was the bureaucrats' target boy despite his stellar success with his patients.

Of course, since he'd vied for the Chairmanship of the Board, they turned up the heat, knowing he championed patient rights for extended medical coverage ... then there was the research. With just days before the election, they were scrambling for anything that might discredit him.

Time had ticked by and, with it, the child's chance of survival. Unable to reach the parents, Peter made an executive decision based on documents he'd received, authorizing medical intervention in their absence.

If the operation failed, Peter could be embroiled in a lawsuit, or worse, a malpractice suit. It would annihilate his life's work and his future. But there was no alternative. He'd tightened his jaw and scrubbed up for surgery.

Now, he dragged himself from the car and cool air smacked him in the face. He stumbled up the steps to the front door. After two attempts, he fit the key in the lock, stepped inside, and closed the door quietly behind him.

He paused, adjusting his eyes to the shadows, then walked to the den. A cup of hot coffee would hit the spot.

Peter rolled his shoulders to knock the kink from his muscles and, tossing his briefcase on the armchair, flopped on the sofa.

"Yikes!" Startled awake, Ellie swung her arms at him.

"What the—" Peter bolted from the cushions.

"Peter." Woozy, Ellie pushed hair off her face and blinked at him.

Moonlight filtering through the crack in the curtains sliced through the darkness in the room.

"Ellie." He shrugged from his jacket and tossed it across the room in the vicinity of the armchair. "Sorry, I didn't know you were here."

A seductive siren. Hair mussed, sweater riding low and exposing the smooth curve of her shoulder, the neckline dipped, giving him a glimpse of the swell of her breasts. A stab of emotion pierced him. She stretched, and he viewed more; that had him nearly buckling over. He took a step closer, wanting to ravish her with his mouth, his hands, his body—Of course, he couldn't. If he did, he'd lose her for sure. He heaved a breath that ripped through him, then hurled from his lungs like a grenade.

"You look awful." She stifled a yawn and, wiggling, pulled the wool cover from beneath her legs.

"Gee, thanks." He plopped down on the corner of the sofa, a wry twist to his mouth.

"What happened?" She rubbed sleep from her eyes.

"An eight-year-old was flown in from a ball camp in San Francisco." He rubbed the bridge of his nose and shut his eyes, easing the sting. "A freak accident."

"And?"

"Might lose him." He lifted her legs onto his lap, stroking. And me with him, he thought. He had wielded the scalpel with a precision that only came from years of experience. Even with that, he prayed he'd made the incision at the correct spot, the first time. Perspiration oozed from every pore in his body and settled on his forehead. He'd get no second try. Tense minutes, hours, ticked by while he stood beneath the bright lights of the operating theater, the boy so still beneath his hands.

"That bad?"

"Acute brain trauma from intracranial hemorrhage."

A long, quiet moment passed between them.

"Kid leaped to make a save and rammed into the goal post, his head snapped back, smashing against the wood. X-rays showed pressure, large spot on the brain. Bleeding. Had to operate. Fast."

Prickles of premonition erupted on Ellie's nape, but she remained quiet, allowing him to vent his distress. For the first time, he was actually sharing something of his work with her. A glimmer of hope for them? Uncertain, she refused to read anymore into it than what it was. Him expressing his concern for his patient.

"Would take a miracle to pull the kid through."

"I believe in miracles, Peter." She brushed his sleeve with her fingertips, the deep lines of strain on his face tearing at her heart.

"Do you, Ellie?" He took her hand and planted a light kiss on her palm.

"Yes." The one word, a soft caress between them.

"Wish I could." He drew her into his arms and pressed his lips to her temple.

She wrapped her arms around him, stroking the nape of his neck, wanting him, comforting him, and feeling the fever rising between them. His mouth slid down her cheek to her lips, his tongue penetrated, tasting her, giving, taking. He deepened the kiss and her tongue sought his, stroking, soothing him. Endless moments later, he glided his hands around her midriff and upward, cupping her breasts.

She moaned with pleasure, her nipples straining against the material of her sweater. He moved his mouth to the hollow of her neck, fanning her skin with his whispered words. "I need—"

She weaved her fingers through his hair and curved into him, signaling her answer.

A shaky breath and Peter scooped her up in his arms, afghan and all. With his mouth still working its magic at the pulse of her throat, he strode from the den and up the stairs to their bedroom.

Chapter 12

Peter kicked the bedroom door open and fell on the bed, holding onto her for a long moment. He began to undress her and the sensual feel of her skin beneath her silk undergarments had him heating up. Breath struggled out of him and perspiration dampened his skin.

It had been so long and here he was on the brink—He flicked the lacy lingerie from her body and pushed her back against the pillows. She lay upon the satin like a goddess. His for the taking. And definitely he would take, sample, and feast on every curve, every shadow, every moist crevice, every luscious inch of her body.

"Peter."

A question or an invitation? He didn't want to go there. Analyze that. So, he didn't answer, couldn't.

She stroked his cheek with her fingertips, and he swallowed the lump of emotion in his throat. He lifted his lashes a fraction and met her gaze. What he glimpsed shook him. Trust for him? Passion for him? Doubts buzzed in his brain and, ruthlessly, he shoved them aside. Hunger gnawed at his insides. He just wanted to feel, touch, taste the heat of her mouth, her skin, her secret places. Almost roughly he took her finger in his mouth, lavishing it with his tongue until she sighed her joy.

This woman he'd married flamed his blood, made his heart pound with such intensity, he could hardly breathe. It was so powerful, this yearning, this feeling that a ripple of fear chased through him. For the first time in his life, he didn't feel in complete control and he was at a loss. And Peter Medeci always had solid command of his life.

Ellie reached to unbutton his shirt, but he stayed her hands, tearing it apart. Then he unbuckled his trousers, tossed them aside, and hauled her against him.

He devoured her with his mouth, his hot breath mingling with hers. Like a man beset by demons that finally found his haven, he plundered her with his tongue, her body with his hands.

Sexual hunger ignited an inferno of the senses. He shifted and his erection pressed against the apex of her thighs. Ellie curved into him and locked her arms around his neck, her fingers weaving a frenzied tempo through his hair. He groaned into her mouth and palmed her breasts, his thumbs flicking her nipples.

Exquisite torture.

Ellie purred her pleasure. A husky breath and he fondled one breast with his fingers while sliding his lips over her chin, down her throat to her cleavage. He lavished her other nipple with his tongue, licking, nipping, and finally pulled it full into his mouth, suckling.

His hand torched its way to her abdomen. He dipped his fingertip in her navel and followed with his mouth. He flicked the shallow crevice with his tongue, his moist fire branding her. She sucked in a breath, and her moan of delight brushed over him like a victory cry.

He stroked lower, his hands gliding across her hips and skirting her mound of curls. Arching into him, Ellie signaled her acceptance, but he continued his quest. He explored her shapely legs, and then took a detour, feathering his fingers across the sensitive arch of her foot. She whimpered and he flamed a path along her inner thigh to her moist folds. A suspended moment and he buried his mouth in her soft curls, his hand following. He slipped his fingers inside her, stroking a magical rhythm until she bucked against his hand.

"Peter," she breathed his name, sensations spiraling inside her, coiling tightly, ready to explode.

He straddled her and inched his mouth up her body until he claimed her lips. He pillaged with his tongue, his hands cupping her buttocks and lifting her to him. A breathless moment, and he slid his steel length inside her, pushing through her slick layers.

Ellie cried his name and, wrapping her limbs around him, pulled him further inside her. He began to move. As his tongue plunged deeper in her mouth, so his shaft plunged deeper into her moist warmth, fusing her to him. With every rhythmic thrust, he rode her deeper, faster, higher into exquisite fervor.

"Ellie, *dio mio*," he gasped into her mouth, catching her pleasured moans with his tongue.

Sexual fever escalated and, with a final thrust, Peter rode her to the pinnacle. Suspended for a killing moment, she shattered against him, and then he caught her there, as wave upon wave of sensation pulsed through him. When the spasms eased, he pressed her head upon his heart and a kiss upon her temple. She cuddled into him and he drew the sheet over them both.

"Peter …"

"Shh." He shut his eyes and stroked her hair, his breathing shaky.

"Peter," she said again, his name a whisper from her lips. But he was already asleep in her arms, the sound of his breathing the only ruffle in the quiet. She lay close by his side, the afterglow of their lovemaking like a halo around her. A sense of peace filled her heart. How fleeting it would be, she'd know soon enough.

Endless seconds ticked by and, finally, Ellie drifted off to sleep.

* * *

"No! Scalpel. No! Incision, here!"

Frantic words crashed through early dawn, startling Ellie awake. Gently, she shook her husband's shoulder. "Peter."

Disoriented, he opened his eyes, and then slammed them shut, concealing his confusion.

"You were having a bad dream."

"Sorry." He shoved both hands through his hair. "Didn't mean to wake you."

He took a deep breath, then the air hurled from him like a miniature tornado. Drawing her closer, he nuzzled her neck, her scent a turn-on. He raised his head and met her eyes, drowsiness making them a darker brown.

Uncertainty jabbed his gut. Would she pull away from him?

A heart rending moment and relief coursed through him.

She smiled and stroked his stubbly cheek with her fingers. Wrapping her arms around him, she pulled him to her bosom. While he dallied there with his mouth, he slid his leg between hers, his coarse hair grazing her flesh. A kittenish growl, and she pushed him back against the pillows, straddling his hips.

"Ellie?"

"It's my turn, husband."

If she had this one last time with him, then she'd make every moment count. She married him for better or worse and she was banking on the former. Dare she bare her soul and unlock her heart to him, once again? Insecurities plagued. She felt like she was falling to earth without a net and fear stabbed her heart.

Heaven or hell? She'd know by morning which it would be.

She glided her fingers across the ripcord strength of his back and pressed her lips to his shoulder. A flick of her tongue, and she tasted the salty sweat of his skin. A low growl and he framed her breasts with his hands. She gasped her delight and arched her back, exposing the fullness of her bosom to his touch. He grunted with pleasure. He brushed her nipples with his thumbs, licked with his tongue, nipped with his teeth, and pulled first one breast into his mouth, then the other.

An aching moment when she pulled back, then knowing he wanted more, pressed her breasts center stage upon his chest. She brushed against him. His chest hair stimulated her nipples, and she bit her lip as erotic sensation pierced her. She raised herself a fraction and splayed her hands across his torso, working her way upward to his nipples, touching, teasing, caressing. She took a shy bud in her mouth, laved it to erection, and Peter jerked beneath her. He signaled he was rock-hard, but Ellie continued her playful antics across his chest. She took the other nipple in her mouth, swirled her tongue around it, licking to and fro, nipping it with her teeth.

"Woman—"

She shut him up by capturing his mouth with her own and teasing it open with her tongue. A heartbeat, and he took charge, holding her head to the spot and plundering her mouth with his.

While his tongue mated with hers, Ellie reached down and found his solid length. She took him in her hand, stroking him base to tip, and he surged, filling her palm.

He groaned his throbbing need, his hands tightening over her shoulders. "You gonna kill me."

"Shh."

Sitting astride him, she guided his sex between her folds and began to ride him. Friction drove him deeper inside her, heating nerves to high-pitch fervor. A guttural sound shot from deep inside him. He cupped her derriere and pushed her further down upon his shaft, his hungry gaze feasting on her breasts. Then, his eyes strayed a notch higher and locked with hers.

Vulnerability and passion charged between them and time suspended.

A high-wattage moment and Ellie lowered her lashes, riding him to the crest. He matched her rhythm, tension coiling and detonating inside him. Her name burst from his mouth at the same moment she cried out his name.

After their breathing regulated, Peter brushed a curl from her moist brow and stroked her shoulder, his heart battering his chest. Still joined to her, he cast her a sexy smile and maneuvered her on her back. "Wife," he breathed against her lips, his tongue plunging deep inside her mouth, the instant his steel length plunged deeper inside her.

Chapter 13

Ellie fluttered her eyelashes open to the sound of the Santa Ana winds whipping the Los Angeles area. The windowpane rattled. She snuggled into warm blankets and blushed, remembering their lovemaking through the night. A contented sigh slipped from her mouth. She turned, reaching for him and grasped a long-stemmed rose nestled on the indentation of his pillow. Disappointment wove through her heart. She picked up the flower and brushed the petals across her lips. Last night, their mind-boggling sexual play had been just another habitual echo in their marriage.

Love her, leave her.

History had merely been repeating itself, and she'd fallen for it hook, line, and sinker. Yet, she'd wanted to comfort him from his grueling day at the clinic. Comfort had quickly turned to desire, escalating to fervor of the senses. Heat assaulted her body and her heart missed a beat. She shut her eyes tight and took a deep breath. She refused to play second fiddle to his medical profession any longer. Nor tiptoe around her passion for a singing career. A sharp exhale and she lifted her lashes. Nope. She'd been there, done that. No more.

She cringed. While she contemplated her life, Peter was at the hospital trying to save that little boy. Guilt grazed her conscience and she sent up a prayer for the child.

Blinking moistness from her eyes, she tossed the rose on the dresser and the rumpled sheets aside. She'd change the bed linen and plunk the flower in water later. Getting up, she trudged to the bathroom. His soap scent, fresh as the outdoors, filled every molecule of air. Damp towels hung haphazardly on a chrome bar and another lay crumpled on the floor, evidence of his quick shower and exit. She sighed and, gathering them up, dropped them in the laundry bin in the corner. Then she turned on the shower, checked the temperature with her hand, and stepped beneath the spray. Steam swirled around her, soothing her tense muscles.

Twenty minutes later, Ellie stood in the middle of the foyer, the quietness of the mansion pressing in on her. She rushed outdoors, checked on King, and hurried straight back to the kitchen. A quick glance at the calendar taped to the refrigerator confirmed her calculations.

Three days left.

Ellie nibbled her bottom lip. She and Peter were headed for an explosive confrontation, especially since last night and the Doc conducting business as usual. However, she'd preempt that inevitability by putting her own plan into action. She'd make a last-ditch effort to save their marriage … give to him what she'd been wanting from him. She'd give him herself. Not sex. More than that. She'd give him intimacy.

Her palms became sweaty and her pulse fluttered. Last night, he had it his way. Tonight, she'd do it her way. She'd risk it all by playing her card one final time. Because she deserved it … he was worth it … and the marriage demanded it. A jitter shot through her. She could lose. She dismantled the doubt by setting her plan in motion.

Several hours later, Ellie was clambering out of a taxi.

"Celebrating?" the cabby asked, unloading bags onto the veranda.

"Hope so," she murmured, trying to shake off the uncanny vibe that someone had been stalking her during her shopping spree.

The man cast her a perplexed look and scratched his head. "Need help with these inside?"

"No, thank you." She gave him a generous tip. "I can manage."

Grinning from ear to ear, he jumped into the driver's seat. "Yes, ma'am."

After Ellie took the groceries into the kitchen, she took a moment to catch her breath. She giggled at her foolishness ... stalker indeed. She watched too much television. That was the problem. She shook off the uneasy feeling and concentrated on the evening ahead.

With a lilting tune upon her lips, she got to work.

By dinner time, and she purposely planned it late to accommodate Peter's schedule, she was feeling like a kid with a new toy. In anticipation, she twirled around the kitchen, her cherry-red dress swishing about her legs.

"Mmm, smells delish." She raised the lid from the pot on the stove, peeked inside, and smacked her lips. "The man won't know what hit him."

Herbs and garlic, olive oil, and tomato-sauce flavors filled the kitchen.

The grilled chicken breasts were smothered in sauce, waiting to be mounted onto a plate of steaming pasta.

She walked over and patted the place settings on the table. She'd chosen midnight blue, Peter's favorite color. The plates and silverware glittered. The crystal goblets sparkled. A bottle of Pinot Noir, flanked by two candles, took center stage.

A good meal and an attentive wife worked wonders for a man stumbling in from a hard day's work. A dash of feminine wiles wouldn't hurt either. She chuckled and then quickly sobered. Relentless in his pursuit, Peter squeezed double into each work hour compared with the average guy. She wished she understood what drove him so. A wistful sigh filtered from her. About to walk from the kitchen, she glanced at the digital clock on the stove's panel.

Six o'clock.

Ellie strolled to the living room, plopped on the sofa, and picked up the remote. Leery of invites to parties and Country Club dos, which would be more for assuaging curiosity regarding her recent absence, she dismissed the idea of calling to chat with her acquaintances. She couldn't call them friends, since most belonged to Peter's medical circle. While little bro was at soccer camp, her parents had flown to Washington, D.C. for a weekend getaway, and nixed that line of communication. She flipped channels instead.

A variety show caught her attention and when it ended, the grandfather clock in the foyer chimed the hour.

Eight o'clock.

Humming a tune, Ellie strolled back to the kitchen and filled a pot with water. She set it on the stove to boil, adding a dash of salt and a drop of olive oil. When steam rose, she opened a package and dumped the noodles in the water. While they cooked, she lit the candles and skimmed the table. She wanted it perfect when Peter walked through the door at eight-thirty.

But something was missing. She snapped her fingers. Snatching salt-and pepper-shakers from the cupboard, she set them on the table. What else? She crinkled her brow. Aha! She dashed up the stairs and back again. Since the vase wouldn't fit, she took the rose and laid it on the tablecloth.

Next, she checked the pasta. Turning off the heat, she strained the noodles and placed them in a large bowl on the counter.

"Five minutes." She wiped her damp palms on her thighs. "Stop being so nervous," she chided herself. "It's just a dinner for your husband."

Yes, but except for simple fare, like breakfast, she'd never done it before. Marta always had control of the kitchen and shooed her out.

"Suppose it backfired, or she put too much salt in the water or overcooked the vermicelli." She wasn't the greatest cook. If anything, her cooking skills were elementary. But she had the enthusiasm, if that counted for anything. She forked a noodle, wrapped it around the tongs, and put it in her mouth. "Just right." She sighed in relief.

The grandfather clock struck the half hour, startling her. Eight-thirty.

"There's more riding on this than a nice meal." She tossed the fork in the sink, then picked it up and put it in the dishwasher.

Her marriage and her future were on the line. Could she pull it off? Would she win the battle of wills between husband and wife? Male and female? Or would it be a draw? A storm was brewing between them. Could she accept his terms? Could he accept hers? And if he didn't?

"Lighten up, Ellie." Nervous laughter mingled with her words. "A rollicking good time with her sexy hubby was in the works." Her laughter turned into a guffaw. "If only that's all there was to marriage." She tapped the counter with her fingers. If it fell flat, she'd be no worse off than three months ago when she walked out. Taming her laughter into a smile, she determined to make the most of their evening.

Minutes ticked by. She puttered around the kitchen, straightening canned goods, rearranging packages in the pantry, then the canisters all in a row on the counter. She inspected everything on the table for the third time.

Glancing up, she caught her reflection in the windowpane and patted her hair in place. Once again, she peeked in the pan and picked up the shakers. She changed her mind and slammed them back on the table. "Stop it."

The clock struck the hour. Nine o'clock.

Her heart plummeted. Maybe he was running late. She ought to know his *modus operandi* by now.

She poked the pasta with her forefinger. "Yech!" She dumped it in the sink and washed it down the garbage disposal. Next, she rinsed the bowl and placed it on the drain-board. She'd make a fresh batch when he got home. Yeah, right. Like at midnight. Or two a.m.

She blew out the candles and plodded to the living room to watch more TV. She couldn't handle a novel right now. Too restless. One day, she'd pen these experiences into a ballad, but not tonight. A sitcom, though, might help chase away her disappointment.

The clock ding-donged the next hour.

Ten o'clock.

Ellie watched *Comedy One.*

The clock struck again.

Eleven o'clock.

Ellie tuned in to *Detectives.* Big mistake. It didn't do anything for her mood.

The clock chimed another hour.

Midnight.

Ellie viewed a romantic comedy. Another miss. She laughed, but then she cried, even though it had a happy ending. What of her?

The clock sounded again.

One a.m.

Ellie clicked the remote off and grabbed the magazine from the coffee table. It was *Family Time* and she leafed through it. Wouldn't you know? They were doing a story on how to survive divorce. She hurled it across the room. Groaning, she kicked off her pumps, stretched out on the couch, and flung her arm across her eyes.

The opening and closing of the front door awoke her. She froze, breath suspended in her throat. Exhaling, she took a moment to balance her feelings. She glanced at the gold-framed clock on the mantel above the fireplace. She winced.

Two a.m.

Ellie swung her legs onto the floor, stood still for a second and trudged out to the foyer. "Good evening ... er ... should I say good morning, Doc?"

He swung around. "Ellie, what're you doing up so late?"

"I thought you might be hungry."

A grin split his tired mouth. "You might say that." He tossed his briefcase on the stand beneath the mirror, shrugged from his overcoat, and draped it on a hook in the alcove. He scooped her up in his arms and took the stairs two at a time.

"I've made—"

"Mmm, you smell good." He nuzzled the nape of her neck, his chin bumping her bead necklace. "Is it that rose thing-a-majig?"

"Actually, it's tomato basil."

He didn't catch it. "And you taste good." He nibbled her earlobe.

"Peter we have to—"

He shoved the bedroom door open with his shoulder. "I know."

"Talk."

He plopped her on the bed then, with his dark gaze never leaving her face, he unbuttoned his shirt, shrugged out of it, and collapsed beside her. He flung his arm around her and hauled her close to his heart. "Boy," he said, his words slurred from exhaustion. "Made it."

"Oh Peter, I'm so glad." She sprang up and kissed him smack on the mouth.

"Me, too." He wrapped his arms around her and pulled her back down beside him. "Can I have another one of those?"

"What?"

"Kiss."

She obliged with a peck on his lips.

He groaned. Bunching her hair in his hands, he pulled her head down and plundered her mouth with his. The kiss was so thorough that when she came up for air, her emotions were tossing.

137

"Miracles happen," he murmured.

"Yes."

He closed his eyes and pressed her head back against his heart. "Yes, they do." He stroked her shoulders.

"I'm wanting to—" she began.

He pushed at the jersey wool of her dress, groping for her breasts.

"I want to tell—" she tried again.

He brought his head to rest in that warm, safe haven of her bosom.

"I'm listening." His words seemed to be low and far away. He snuggled into her even more. "Heaven."

"I wanted to let you know ..." She paused, searching for the right words. Her breath came in quick puffs. "I have to ..." She wiped a tear rolling down her cheek. "As much as I want to, I-I need to—" She stopped.

His steady breathing tickled her cheek. He hadn't heard a word she said. Beat, he'd fallen asleep in her arms.

Another repeat from history.

She traced the grooves of strain from his nose to his jaw, his stubble rough beneath her fingertips. "I do love you, Peter." She shuffled from the bed and stood, watching him. Then, she pulled the light cover over him. "Too much." Her heart cracked. "I-I can't postpone my life any longer." She pressed her fist against her mouth and smothering a sob, fled the room.

Chapter 14

Peter shifted under the sheets. Rain shot against the window and penetrated through his drowsiness. He reached to pull Ellie close to his side and clutched empty space. A groan grated from his mouth. He cracked an eye open and seeing her side of the bed hadn't been slept in, he bolted upright, fully awake.

"Ellie, you in there?" He glanced at the adjoining bathroom, but a sliver of fear pricked his heart. Muttering an oath, he leaped from bed. "Probably in the kitchen, brewing coffee." He forced a smile on his lips as the image played on his mind. He'd walk in, place his hands around her waist and pull her back against his chest. Gradually, he'd slide his hands upward, across her abdomen and higher still, until he cupped her breasts.

While he fondled the prizes in his hands, he'd nuzzle the smooth dip of her collarbone. What if she wasn't there? Doubt pierced his gut. What if she was? He shut up the nemesis in his brain.

After a quick shower, he pulled on jeans and a navy sweater, socks and sneakers, and bounded down the stairs, taking them two at a time. "Ellie!"

No answer.

Maybe she didn't hear him.

"Ellie!" He hurried to the kitchen and his heart sank. He'd known, of course. The unsettling feeling in his gut had tipped him off, but he denied it.

He collapsed on a chair, folded his arms across the table and plunked his head down. The motion rocked the place setting, but he barely noticed. Where had he gone wrong? In a little over three months, she'd left him three times. *What's the plan, Doc*? Shut up!

During these couple of weeks, he thought things had improved between them. Heck, after their dinner date and what followed by the fireside in the den ... a heavy groan erupted from deep within him ... and later in their bedroom ... He couldn't be faulted for thinking things were back to normal.

What had he missed? He worked hard day and night to give her every material thing anyone could want. And she'd never gone hungry—

His thoughts halted and his head shot up.

Tomato basil aroma lingered in the air. He sniffed. A hint of cherry scent from the half-melted candles on the table. A bottle of Pinot Noir, crystal goblets, shiny silverware, a midnight-blue color scheme ... his favorite. He shoved the chair back with such force that it toppled. He stood and glanced around. Had she done all this for him? For them?

He pounded his fist on the table and dishes rattled. What had he done for her? "Loved her, that's what." He pushed his hands through his hair. "And saved a life," he whispered to the stillness in the room. "I chose to save a life instead of partaking in this domestic dinner scene she planned." Air whirled inside his chest to near-explosive proportions. Slowly, he defused the pent-up pressure by exhaling several consecutive breaths.

The magnetic calendar on the refrigerator caught his attention. He narrowed his eyes. They'd agreed on three weeks. He calculated. She owed him two more days. And, by gosh, he was going to collect.

* * *

The storm that had threatened all day, unleashed its vendetta upon the City of the Angels.

Ellie lay curled on the frayed sofa, listening to the wind and rain lash against the window of her little apartment. Chill in the air was beginning to numb her fingers and she wrapped her coat closer about her.

A moan slipped from deep inside her. She blinked several times to accustom her eyes to the shadows. Although every muscle in her body resisted, she managed to drag herself off the couch and slog across the room. She flicked on the light switch by the door. It flickered but stayed on. She breathed a sigh of relief.

A rumble of thunder made her jump. She slapped her hands over her ears, her heart pummeling her chest. "No!"

An uncanny stillness followed. She swallowed her scream on a trembling breath. She was about to take another when the heavens burst open. Thunder detonated. Lightning flashed across the sky, illuminating her standing frozen to the spot in the middle of the floor.

The light flickered and went out.

"Stop! Stop!"

At that moment, the door was flung open and someone hurled through it. "What's the matter?"

Peter's voice shot straight through her fear and into her heart. She swayed, the dark void spinning around her. She groped for anything that would break her fall. Something landed with a thud on the floor, and Peter caught her in his arms. She clung to him and sucked in a mouthful of air.

"Shh, it's all right." Peter brushed hair off her brow, his tone soothing. "I've got you." He drew her closer and she curled in the haven of his arms.

"It's quirky weather," he said, his words seeming to come from miles away. "When did you last eat?"

"I-I-I don't remember." She shivered. "Ye-e-sterday, I think."

"Hmm, didn't we go through this not long ago in this same place?"

She nodded, and her hair fell, shielding her face. "You came here with that giant chocolate Christmas tree."

He chuckled. "You do remember."

"A huh."

"Ellie, I could shake you for not eating." He stroked her shoulders, the small of her back, a half-smile playing on his mouth. "But then, you'd blame my red-blooded Italian heritage again."

An explosion of elements resounded and she leaped against him.

"Hey, it's okay." He lifted her up in his arms, groped his way to the sofa, and sat down, cradling her on his lap.

Tremors shook her body. A tense moment and she wrapped her arms around his neck, locking her hands together. She burrowed her head in his shoulder, his heart thudding against her mouth.

"You've got to eat something." The doctor took over and pried her hands loose.

"Don't want to."

"To think straight," he said.

"I am think—"

"Could've fooled me—"

"I don't think I can cook ... too tired."

"You cooked last night." He hesitated a fraction. "A first-class meal."

"You missed it."

Grim silence. "Yeah."

"Why, Peter?" She glanced up at him, and although her eyes had become accustomed to the darkness, she could barely make out his features.

He tightened his arms around her, communicating his need for her to understand. Understand him. "Because I saved a life, Ellie."

She jerked in his embrace.

"I chose to save a life, instead of making it home on time to have dinner with you."

"I-I see."

"Do you?" he said, tone leaden.

"Yes. Yes, of course." She stroked his breast, rain-damp wool tickling her fingers, the scent permeating through to her. "Absolutely. No question, Peter".

He covered her hand with his. "Glad you finally understand."

Ellie always understood that part of his life. And she'd never ask him to do differently. Never. Guilt and confusion nicked her. *Then why did you leave again?* Because it appeared he didn't include their lives in his heroic crusades.

These three weeks had made it clear. There didn't seem to be a way to balance his unquenchable ambition for success with her desire for a regular home life, and pursuit of her unconventional career. Regret ripped across her heart. Was she asking too much?

"Thank you, Ellie." He shuffled from under her and cupped her cheek, his hand warm and comforting. "Got a candle?"

"In the drawer by the stove," she said, hearing him walk away.

Cold air smacked her where his body heat had kept her warm only moments ago. She curled her legs beneath her coat and rubbed her arms.

A match flared and he set the candle on the counter. "Sorry, I dropped the grocery bags to catch you." He smiled and stooped down to collect the food off the floor. "Fruit and vegetables are sprouting everywhere."

"I'll help you." She made to get up, but he waved her back down.

"I got 'em." He scooped a couple of tomatoes and a celery stalk from the linoleum.

She realized they were items she'd bought for their romantic dinner last night. "I see you found everything all right." She chuckled, a half-hearted sound.

"I did," he said. "Now get ready for an adventure your taste buds won't forget."

She shifted to a more comfortable position on the couch. "Who's cooking?"

"Leave that to me, *principessa*."

A quiet moment slipped by, then she made to get up again. "You don't know—"

"That I do." Gently, he pushed her back against the cushions. "Goes to show how little you know about the man you married."

"You can boil water, I know." She raised a shapely brow, a half-smile tugging at her mouth. "But cook?"

"We Italians are known for our culinary skills." He winked. "Among other things."

"I bet."

He pinned her with a hard look. "Speaking of bets." He set lettuce on the counter, next to the tomatoes and celery. "You owe me two more days."

"You can't be serious, Peter."

"That I am." He opened a cupboard, removed two paper plates, then opened a drawer and took out a knife.

She remained silent for so long, he shot her an accusing gaze.

"Welching on the deal?"

"No."

"You'll pay up?" he asked.

She decided to play along. "Depends on how good a cook you are."

"Blackmail?"

She cast him an innocent look and curved her mouth in a saucy smile, but her heart was breaking.

"Get ready." He tossed a tomato in the air and caught it in the palm of his hand, even in the dim light. "Your taste buds are gonna be rockin.'"

He rocked her world so much, she felt like a toy boat in a

hurricane, emotional tidal waves buffeting her. Her grin turned wistful. "Huh!"

"Hey, remember my Italiano pasta-nasta sauce—"

"Yeah." She grinned. "But I have yet to sample it."

He chuckled and rinsed vegetables under the tap, tore off a paper towel from the wall dispenser, and dried them. "I used to make enough for the whole *famiglia*, then got roped into doing the dishes."

"So you said," she murmured.

"Yeah." He chuckled, but it was a strained sound.

Just a few weeks ago at Christmas, he'd come for her here, wooed her back to the 'castle', and Ellie believed they'd resolved their differences—A sigh whipped from her and she slammed a padlock on those thoughts. She didn't want to go there.

"Christmas every day," she whispered, her tone flippant.

"It could be, Ellie." He turned and ensnared her gaze with his.

She averted her eyes, breaking the connection, and remained silent.

Wind rattled the windowpane.

"So, you can do more than boil water?" She feigned a cough and detoured from the bittersweet memory.

He shuttered his eyes and then tossed the ripe tomato on the counter. "Sure."

"You're kidding." She attempted a grin to lighten the mood, but it faded on her mouth.

"Nope," he murmured.

"But when we visited your family in Rome on the way to our weekend—" She broke off, not wanting to remember the sizzling summer nights on the Mediterranean beach ... the scent of orange blossom mingling with salt tang in the air ... his kisses beneath a full moon.

"Honeymoon," he finished for her.

"Yes," she murmured, pushing up on one elbow, her weight denting the cushion. "Servants bustled in and out of the *palazzo*."

"Hardly that."

"Estate, then—"

"We hadn't always lived like that, Ellie," he said. "In fact, after I was accepted to med school, my folks returned to Italy."

"You stayed."

"And met you." He slanted her an amused glance.

"Yes." She lay back down on the couch and nestled her cheek on her palm. "Why didn't you tell me? I assumed—"

"I wanted to impress you."

"You did."

"I did?"

"Mmm."

He smiled, then sobered. "How do you think I put myself through medical school?"

She sized him up from head to toe. "Modeling? Calendar pin-up?" She crinkled her brow, then her eyes lit up. "A bouncer at the neighborhood pub."

He laughed. "Ellie Ross Medeci, you are so wrong."

She raised her brows.

"With my Italian culinary skills," he said. "Waiting tables, getting ti—"

"Tips."

"Yeah," he grumbled.

She snickered. "Among other things."

"On my honor—"

The lights flickered back on, and she blinked, adjusting her focus to the brightness. "Good timing." She glanced from the single bulb on the ceiling to the knife in his hand, poised to slice through the plump tomato. "You were saying?"

"On my honor, they were reserved for a brown-eyed song-bird."

"Really, Peter?"

"The woman doubts me, even after all these years."

"Do not."

He sent her a look that spoke volumes, making her heart flutter. Bittersweet memories raced between them. Silence grew thick with emotion, vibrating and sucking them into its vortex.

Then, he made an incision through the tomato with the blade and blood-red juice spurted out.

She sat up and licked her lips. "Why are you here again, Peter?"

He focused on the tip of her tongue. Abruptly he turned, opened the refrigerator, and dumped the remaining groceries inside. He closed it with a tad more force than necessary. "I thought you might be hungry."

"Oh, really." Trust him to say something like that and throw her pulse into a scramble. She drank him in with her gaze. Raindrops glistened on his hair, dampness on his shoulders, and strain on his features. She frowned.

"Yeah." He scrunched the brown-paper bag into a ball and hurled it in the sink in such a careless manner she thought she must've imagined tension on his face. Picking up the shakers, he sprinkled salt and pepper on the tomatoes and slapped on the second bread slice.

"You're wet."

He shrugged. "You must be cold." He glanced around and spotted the gas heater on the wall. "That thing still not working?"

"I don't know." Her eyes never left his face.

He turned away and fiddled with a knob. "That should do it."

"You're doing it again." She grabbed a cushion, hugging it to herself.

"Taking care of you?"

She sighed. Taking over was what she'd meant to say, but he *was* taking care of her. Since the day she met him, he'd done that. He even used his overseas contacts to help her father land the professorship in Sussex. Even at the beginning of his career, he always made sure she had all the material comforts money could buy. He'd given her everything except the one thing she wanted most.

"Why did you come here, Peter?" she grilled him.

"Italians are noted for their staying power and family tradition, remember." The heater flared at that moment and nearly drowned out his words.

"Are they?"

"No." He hoisted himself up from his haunches and faced her, his tone glib. "I made it up."

He grabbed the sandwich platter and soda can off the counter and plopped them on the table beside her. Then, he hauled her into his arms and smothered her with kisses.

She gripped his shoulders, her insides in turmoil. His magnetism was so potent, she fisted her hands to gain strength and maintain her ground. When she came up for air, she said, "They are also noted for taking their women for granted."

"Not true." He dropped a kiss on the tip of her nose.

"We like being good providers and sometimes we can't be as attentive as women want."

"Like me?"

"You wanted me attentive, Ellie?"

She wanted to clobber him. "No. I just wanted you for sex."

He lifted a black brow and amusement glinted in his eyes. "I trudge home after seventeen hours on the clock, you entice me to bed, and fool around with me."

Her mouth twitched at the corners. Oh, he was very good at turning the tables on her. "A wife's right," she tossed back.

"And a husband's." He pressed his lips to her forehead. "Now, eat your sandwich." He propelled her onto the couch, picked up the platter from the counter and placed it in her hands.

She screwed up her face. "I thought you said you could cook."

"This is the appetizer."

"Hmm." She didn't miss the double entendre in his words.

He shed his coat and plunked down beside her. Eating his own sandwich, he glanced her way to make sure she was munching hers.

She picked at the cheese from between the bread slices, popped a piece in her mouth and forced it down. Their conversation felt like the lull before the storm.

"Why did you marry me?" he fired at her.

She took a sip of soda, then set it on the floor, desperately trying to ignore emotion tossing inside her. "What a thing to ask."

"Answer the question."

She quirked an eyebrow and set the half-eaten sandwich on the plate teetering on the arm of the couch.

He took the last swig of his drink, plunked the can beside hers on the floor and turned, his gaze searching.

"Don't you know?" she asked.

"You said for money."

"That was to bug you."

"You did," he said.

He waited.

She made him wait.

He mocked a cough.

"You swept me off my feet."

"And you left again." He reached over and set his plate on the counter, and then rubbed his palms over his denim-clad thighs. "Why?"

"I had to think," she murmured. "I thought it would shake you from your complacency."

"Think?" He lifted himself from the sofa and loomed over her. "I work like a dog to keep you in style, give you what you want, and you think me complacent?"

"You give me everything I want Peter, except the one thing I want most."

"What's that?" he bit out.

"We went through this at Christmas," she murmured. "But apparently you missed it."

"Tell me again," he commanded.

"You," she said, the word a thread of sound, but he caught it. He shook his head, baffled. "I married you. You've got me. Period."

"I have your name and your status, Peter." She bolted up straight. "You, I catch between flights and medical events."

"And saving lives," he added, his tone dry. "We've gone through this before, Ellie."

"Yes." She folded her hands in her lap, not wanting him to witness her trembling. Her reaction wasn't so much from the storm raging outside, but from the one about to explode between them. Already on precarious ground, they were inching toward the precipice. "What about the casualty in our lives?"

"What do you mean?"

"Practice what you preach."

He squinted.

"You, me, our marriage," she explained.

He shoved a hand through his hair. He thought she understood a neurosurgeon's rigorous schedule—his goals, his determination to succeed beyond the norm. He thought she'd stand by him all the way. Perspiration glazed his brow, a stone in his gut. He wanted to give her everything. Everything he hadn't had as a child. Make her happy. A sigh worked its way out from deep in his throat. Obviously, it hadn't worked. "You want a stay-at-home husband, Ellie?"

"Of course not."

"Then what's the problem?"

She hooked a stray hair behind her ear. "You wanting a stay-at-home wife is what's the problem."

"Why's that a problem?"

"Because I want to do more than schmooze my time away, use my talents—"

"Ahh. Singing the blues is what you're after."

"Anything wrong with that?"

"We had an agreement."

"It's over tomorrow."

"So it is." His jaw went rigid.

"You understand why I left?" she asked, tilting her chin.

"No."

"I became so enmeshed in the demands of being the *dottore's* wife that I lost myself. My identity."

"You thought you'd find it in *The Blue Room*?"

She swooped up her cap from the sofa and threw it at him. "What if I did?"

It sailed over his head. He caught it, his laser-sharp gaze never leaving her face. "Did you?"

"You made sure I didn't," she muttered, her words tinged with resentment.

"A necessary political maneuver."

"And tomorrow? And the day after? Next month? Next year? What?" she blurted, words tumbling from her mouth. "There's always going to be another political challenge in the medical field for you to vault over."

"For good cause."

"Yes, I know," she hurled back, her heart sinking. "But at whose expense?"

"Have I missed something here?"

She sighed. "Maybe I have."

Must he forfeit all and give in to her conditions? How could he survive this marriage when his relentless drive propelled him forward to succeed for her, for them ... and she was smothering him with her domestic demands?

"No." He shook his head. "Possibly we both have."

She nodded, the silence thick and murky between them.

"You want me to dance to your tune in *The Blue Room*?"

"Yes ... no. I mean ..." She collapsed back on the sofa and drew her coat closely about her. She had sacrificed her dreams for her parents. After five years, must she still continue to forfeit her dreams, now for her husband? How could she survive this marriage, when he was stifling her with his professional commands, except when she was in his arms?

"I want to be more than a recurring one-night stand."

"What?" He shot her an incredulous look.

She trailed her fingers down the row of buttons on her coat. "Slam-bam-thank-you-ma'am nights when you can squeeze me into your tight schedule, does not a marriage make."

He glared at her.

She glared right back.

"You thought that?"

"Yes."

"All the time?"

"Most of it."

"Why didn't you say something?"

"I tried," she murmured. "But soon as your head hit the pillow, you were out for the count."

He placed his hands over hers, stopping the bumpy ride of her fingers over the buttons. "I'm listening now."

Moisture pressed against her eyelids. He was doing it again. Turning her insides to mush. She swallowed, took a deep breath and exhaled. "I … uh—"

His cell phone beeped.

A knowing gaze passed between them, seeming to seal the fate of their marriage.

He pulled the mobile from his coat pocket and flipped it open. "Medeci." A scowl, then he paled. "On my way."

Chapter 15

Ellie climbed out of the cab, tipped the cabbie, and long after he drove off, she stood staring at the mansion. In the background, King barked, but it didn't faze her. Her emotions seemed to have fled, leaving a big hole inside her.

After Peter had hurled himself from her apartment, she decided to return and collect the remainder of her things from the 'castle'. But first, she'd make good on her end of the deal by spending the last night in her own room. Peter would be at the hospital for the rest of the day, night, and a good part of the next morning, so no danger of bumping into him. By then, the tug-o-war between them would be over.

And the winner?

She laughed, a raw sound. Nobody won in a marriage breakup.

Her shoulders sagged. A deep sigh, and she trudged up the stairs to the front door. Just as she was fitting the key in the lock, the door flew open.

"*Senora* Medeci, hurry!" Marta waved her hands about, motioning her to come inside.

"What's wrong?" Ellie asked. "Is it your sister again?"

The housekeeper shook her head, speed-waddling to the living room. "My sister and her husband, okay." A glimmer of a grin on her mouth. "No *problema*. I fix."

"Good to hear."

Marta's grin vanished. "I just come in and hear news."

Ellie turned to the television. Breath jammed in her throat, her heart seeming to stop before going full throttle. Peter's mugshot was splashed across the screen amidst a media frenzy in front of St. Joseph's Hospital.

In a daze, she heard the newscaster report, "Dr. Peter Medeci, better known as 'the renegade Doc' in medical circles, could have written his own prescription for a quick demise." A snicker. "He's pushed his luck by administering treatment to a family member. Although not a direct violation of the Code of Medical Ethics, it is considered a major *faux pas* that could land him in front of the firing squad. Disciplinary measures could tarnish his stellar reputation, cost him his *coup d'etat* as Chairman of the Medical Board and suspend his medical license."

Ellie gripped the back of the couch, her other hand flying to her temple. She did a quick calculation. When she'd been admitted to the emergency for treatment after her fall, Peter had relinquished her to another doctor. She frowned. Surely that couldn't be what this was about. Another image flashed through her mind and made fine hair stand on end all over her body.

"… a new development in the story," the newscaster's voice filtered to her. "Stay tuned, we'll fill you in after the commercial."

Ellie swayed. "Oh no!" The knowingness of what she suspected rammed her in the stomach and she nearly doubled over.

"Tea?" Marta asked, wringing her hands on her apron.

Ellie shook her head, chills frosting her flesh. Dear God, what had she done? "I have to go to him."

"*Que?*"

"I have to get to the hospital."

* * *

154

After battling the nightmarish rush-hour traffic on the Golden State Freeway in Los Angeles, Jose swerved in front of the hospital, the limo's wheels squealing.

Ellie leaped out and shoved her way through the throng of media hecklers, questions flying at her from every which way. A sliver of panic pierced her, but she squashed it. Her role as the doctor's wife for the past five years held her in good stead. Ignoring their relentless interrogation, she ran up the steps and into the hospital lobby.

She breathed a sigh of relief. Compared to the frenzy outside, the lobby was quiet. She made a beeline for Peter's office, but it was closed. She rushed back to the front desk. "Joey Ross' room, please."

"Are you a relation?" the receptionist asked.

"Yes," Ellie nearly screamed the word.

"No one by that name." The woman glanced up from her computer monitor.

"Are you sure?" Ellie gulped down trepidation. "Joseph Ross."

The receptionist hit the keyboard and squinted at the screen. "There's a Joseph Rods in Room 203."

"Tha-ank you." Ellie dashed down the corridor to the elevator, perspiration beading her upper lip.

Moments later, she skidded to a halt outside Room 203 and tried to catch her breath. Soft music drifted to her from inside. She licked her lips and walked in.

"Ellie, darling," her mother said, her voice trembling. "We just got in and were about to call you."

"Our plane got snowed at Kennedy International Airport." Her father stepped away from the bed to give her a hug, his words gruff. "Telephone lines down. A real mess." He brushed a hand across his eyes, visibly moved. "That husband of yours took care of it, though."

A tremor zapped through Ellie. Her little brother was half-hidden beneath the sheets, his head swathed in bandages. A

CD player on the window ledge cooed a soothing melody. "Why didn't you tell me he was at the ball camp in San Francisco?"

"He wanted to surprise you—" her mother murmured, her voice breaking.

"How is he?" The words scraped her throat. "Where's Peter?"

"Joey's got a tough noggin." Her father tapped his own head with his knuckles, but the crack in his voice was unmistakable. "Peter went to make a statement and put a lid on that racket out there."

Ellie propped her hip on the bed. "Hey, slugger." Bending closer, she placed a kiss on her little brother's pale cheek.

"Uncle Peter promised to come back," Joey whispered, his words wobbled from the sedative.

"I'll go find him." Emotion lodged in her throat as she watched him close his eyes and drift off to sleep.

Ellie stepped outside the room and leaned her head back against the wall, swiping at a tear slipping beneath her lashes.

How could she have been so naïve as to think she and Peter could live an ordinary life? It could never be just about them. It was bigger than the both of them. His profession, his research, his political aspirations, and, most of all, his patients. She choked back a sob. Peter's skill had saved her little brother.

"You dolt!" she chastised herself.

Peter had driven himself at a ruthless pace to be at the top of his game, to make a difference in people's lives. One of those people had turned out to be Joey. The other was her ... providing for her, ensuring she didn't want for anything. She sucked in several shaky breaths and hurried along the corridor to the lift. Even when he stumbled through the front door of their home, too tired to talk, too tired to eat, he was never too tired to hold her, love her.

The elevator opened on the main floor and Ellie stepped out, hurrying down the hallway. She stopped in front of his office door, *Peter Medeci, M.D., Neurosurgery*. Her heart thumped. She swiped her damp palms on her coat, brushed a stray hair off her brow and knocked.

"Come in," Peter's gruff voice sounded from within, and her pulse leaped.

She pushed the door open and allowed it to click behind her. "Why didn't you tell me?"

"Ellie." He glanced up from writing in a file, the deep grooves on his face reflecting the extreme stress he'd been under. "I didn't know."

"How could you not know?" She took several more steps that brought her to the edge of his desk.

"His head was bandaged," he said, a muscle boxing his jaw. "I didn't recognize him." He slapped his hands on the desk with such force, the pen between his fingers flew across the room and made Ellie jump. Hauling himself from the chair, he turned to contemplate the Los Angeles skyline through the wide expanse of glass making up one whole wall.

"Explain." She caught her bottom lip between her teeth to keep it from quivering.

"After five years, a three-year-old becomes virtually a stranger."

"Especially when you don't see him during that time."

"Yeah."

A tense moment assaulted the air between them.

"There was a typo," Peter bit out. "Rods instead of Ross on his admittance form." He turned to confront her, every muscle in his body seeming to stiffen. "I was the only neuro on duty, had to move fast, make a decision—"

"Shh." She shoved down a whimper.

For a smart woman, who didn't feel too savvy right now, she'd almost made the biggest blooper of her life. Her husband was in a class by himself. She should have understood him better; his arduous work schedule, pressure of his chosen profession, his dedication.

She could hardly breathe. She knew that without Peter, her own dream would be insignificant.

"How-w is he?" she asked, to cover the revealing moment.

"Stable," he said. "He's already bidding to play the championship game."

"Takes after his uncle." A wobbly smile. "I heard the newscast—"

"Hot air and pipe steam." Peter strode around the wide girth of glossy mahogany, grabbed her by the shoulders, and stared her straight in the eye. "I was ethically bound to administer treatment." He flicked a curl on her shoulder with his index finger. "Everything's documented, your parents have signed an affidavit, and I'll be transferring Joey to another physician as soon as it's practical."

"Someone leaked the story to the press," she murmured.

"I suspect the former Chair and his lackies," he muttered. "A high-profile case, a hint of impropriety and the media goes nuts."

"A wife working the clubs during this crucial election would've played right into their hands, further assassinating your character." She shuddered to think what might have happened if he hadn't found her in time.

"They got nothing. *Niente*," he bit out. "Louie was willing to part with the photos for a hefty sum."

She gasped. "There were photos?

He nodded, his gaze fixed on her face.

"Of me?"

He hedged.

"What?" A shiver shot up her spine. She remembered Louie's 'publicity' shots, then a camera flashing when she'd taken King for a walk, and later, the uncanny feeling that someone was stalking her while she was shopping. "Bad?"

"The high-tech revolution and digital cams make it easy to alter, tamper—"

"No!" She groaned.

"I got 'em before he cut a deal with the *mole* who was ready to dish them to the Trades."

"I-I-I was the decoy?"

"Yeah." He steeled his jaw. "They were going to get to me by flashing you in compromising poses on the front page of every newspaper in the country. Days prior to the election, it would've annihilated me and—"

"Me." Her knees buckled, and Peter tightened his grip on her arms. She gulped down bile rising in her throat. He'd been trying to protect her … them, and she thought—

"You won the Chair."

He nodded.

"When?"

"Final count came in yesterday." A grin skimmed his mouth, then disappeared.

"Congrats." Yesterday, she had skipped out on him when they should've been celebrating, yet he'd made time to come find her again. Remorse grazed her heart. "And your license?"

"Intact." Noting her pale features, Peter wondered if their marriage would be intact come tomorrow.

"You couldn't afford to lose." She turned her head and a wave of golden-brown curls fell over her face, camouflaging her features. "You have too much at stake."

"That's right." He almost scowled. Where had her sparkle, her laughter gone? He couldn't blame it all on today's events.

A moment, and the sledgehammer found its mark, sending his heart ramming against his ribs. Was he any better than Louie and his cronies? Yes, he saved lives. He couldn't do otherwise. But he also promised to cherish Ellie above all others; yet could his relentless ambition to succeed—career, goals, money, power have been destroying her emotionally and psychologically? He was dumbfounded at the possibility.

On a 24/7/365 work schedule, he'd been alienating her from

his life without realizing it. *You buffoon!* She'd been trying to communicate to him that his preoccupation with his profession was eroding their marriage, and he thought—

He broke out in a sweat. In just a few hours she could be gone from his life. Without Ellie, his success was meaningless.

Wrapping his arms around her, he placed his chin on the crown of her head and heaved a deep breath. A double whammy, Doc. He exhaled in force. Not recognizing the 'miracle boy' as his eight-year-old brother-in-law had also knocked him for a loop. Regret ripped through him. He should've given more attention to his family … to Ellie.

For a brilliant man, who racked his brains to find a solution to problems in his marriage, he'd almost blown it sky-high. A growl built in his throat. *Physician, heal thyself.*

"Peter, thank you for saving Joey's life," Ellie murmured, stroking the breast pocket of his lab coat.

"It's my job."

"I know." She fiddled with the bead necklace at her throat that Peter had given her so long ago; she'd always worn it—a reminder of their life before it had gotten so complicated. "But if you'd come for dinner, if you weren't so dedicated, if you weren't still at the hospital that night—"

"But I was, Ellie." He brushed her chin with his knuckles. "I could say the same thing."

"What d' you mean?" She nipped her lip with her teeth.

He focused on her mouth. A beat and, "If you hadn't stood by me, if you hadn't left the club, if you hadn't agreed to play the good doctor's wife in the nick of time—"

"But I did." Ellie linked her arms around his neck and held on to him tightly. He felt good, strong … sexy.

"Exactly," he said, his words nearly drowned out by nature's fury ravaging the land.

Ellie gazed out the window at the freak storm pummeling Los Angeles. What had been a drizzle, turned into a full-fledged

160

downpour, lashing against the window like an overdue wake-up call. Even the southern California sunshine couldn't be taken for granted.

In a world where everyone searched for 'the one', she and Peter had found each other. A miracle in itself. She blinked moisture stinging her eyes. Precisely why their bedroom play was like a drug, a love potion flowing from her heart into his. A true love. A divine gift.

"Question is …" Peter mocked a cough.

Her attention on alert.

"Are you still willing to stand by your man?"

She slanted him a flirty gaze. "Mmm, for a sampling of your infamous pasta-nasta dish, I could stay in your corner."

He tossed his head back and laughed.

But she wasn't done. "Aaand you know what they say?"

He hiked a jet-black brow.

"Beside every successful man stands a woman."

He grinned. "I bet that could work the other way too."

She squinted at him. "Hmm."

"We had a deal, remember?"

"Yes, but that's over—"

He glanced at the Omega watch on his wrist. "In precisely fourteen hours."

"And?" So he was keeping count.

"I'm giving you what you want."

He wouldn't be so cruel as to bring up divorce at such a time. At least he could wait a few days, after the shock of today's events had worn off.

"What's that?" she ventured to ask.

"A victory celebration."

Her heart lurched.

"In the style of a political rally."

Her pulse picked up tempo. "Your supporters will be expecting it."

Tongue in cheek. "*The Blue Room* sounds like the perfect platform."

She chuckled and then the sound froze on her lips.

"Under new ownership" – he paused for effect – "it should be … uh … a hip place."

She gaped at him.

"A talented, sexy *chanteuse* to belt out a couple of numbers," he said, his gaze fixed on hers, "would pull in the crowds."

"A one-night gig?"

"Might develop into som'm more."

"Won't your constituents turn up their noses?"

An ambulance siren pierced through the elements outside and their banter inside, yet affected neither.

"This is the twenty-first century and medical science is advancing by quantum leaps." Peter brushed his chin with the back of his hand, and his mouth lifted at the corner. "Time to shake up the … uh … what did you call them?"

"Fuddy-duddies."

"Oh, yeah, time to shake the fuddy-duddies from their" – he shot her a look full of meaning – "complacency."

"Sure thing, Doc." She gave him a wide, innocent look, trying to hold back a giggle. She didn't make it.

Peter feigned a frown. "Research data indicates music has healing qualities … activates neurons … endorphins in the brain … feel good … speeds healing." He grinned. "A cap version of findings."

"An experiment, then?"

He shrugged. "The outcome is certain."

She pretended to study her fingernails and then she glanced up and fell into his gaze. Her breath snagged in her throat. "That's only half of what I want."

It was his turn to gape.

"You, my sexy Italian, are what I want most."

He slapped his head in mock surprise. "Yes, well, to get me

lady, you gotta give me more'n those slam-bam-thank-you-buster nights." He smiled.

"I'll see what I can do about squeezing you between my singing gigs."

He was about to object, when the intercom sounded. "Dr. Medeci to the front desk."

He groaned.

On tiptoe, Ellie gave him a quick kiss, adjusted the stethoscope around his neck, and shooed him out. "Duty calls, *dottore*."

He strode to the door. "We'll discuss the details tonight."

"Do they include family and all that jazz?"

"They do … and the global clinic—" but by then he'd slipped out the door.

She stared after him aghast. There was no stopping him. She curved her lips in a cheeky smile. But then, she knew he was no ordinary man … she had indeed married her Prince Charming.

The door opened a crack and he poked his head back inside. "Two a.m. work for you?"

"We'll make it work, my love." She blinked the sheen from her eyes, the rest of her words a silent tempo in her head— 'I'm still *All Wrapped Up in You*.'

"You got a deal, *principessa*." He winked and the door swung behind him.

Out in the corridor, Dr. Peter Medeci heard Ellie humming and paused mid-stride. He blinked moistness from his eyes, the melody wrapping around his heart like a promise. He knew then, he had indeed gotten his own miracle.

Also by Sun Chara

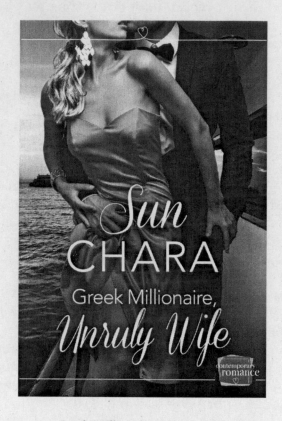

Greek Millionaire, Unruly Wife
Manhattan Millionaire's Cinderella
All Wrapped UP

Printed by RR Donnelley at Glasgow, UK